SCHOOLIES

Derek Pugh

Schoolies
Young Adult Fiction.
The characters in this book are fictitious.
First Published 2019

Text copyright © Derek Pugh 2019
Design and layout by Michael Pugh:
         michael.pugh@bigpond.com

ISBN 978-0-6481421-5-7 : Printed—Paperback
ISBN 978-0-6481421-6-4 : eBook

www.derekpugh.com

A catalogue record for this
book is available from the
National Library of Australia

To Harry and Roy.

Be Schoolies ... but be careful.

1.

If you always sleep under a ceiling fan the moving air becomes necessary to get a good night's sleep— at least in the build-up. I live in Darwin where the air gets so hot and humid, for two or three months every year, that anyone sleeping without a fan risks waking in a pool of sweat. If my fan is turned off, I'll wake before it stops moving, so Mum sometimes gets me out of bed on time just by turning it off. I heard the click of the fan's controller a few minutes ago and have been trying to ignore the still air to get a little more snoozing in. without much success. The switch is near the door, she didn't even have to come in, but now I can hear her shouting down the hall.

"Hurry up, Ras, school starts in half an hour. Don't forget to lock the door." I hear her car start under the house and then she's gone.

I groan, but I am awake now. Our house is an old elevated place with louvre windows. Palm leaves press up against the flyscreens, giving my room a strange green hue in the morning light. Dad and Mum have both gone to work now. My brother Charles, who lives in the granny-flat downstairs, is away at work in the mines. He's an electrician and a 'FIFO', which means he's a fly-in-fly-out worker and we only see him every other week when he comes home after a shift.

I am alone and I have a choice—if I turn the fan back on, I could sleep an extra hour or so, have a leisurely breakfast, and skip school for the morning. Or, I could get up now, have a shower, a quick breakfast, walk to school, which is only five minutes away, and finish year 12. Tough choice, but I do what I always do … I sigh and roll out of bed and head to the shower. Today is the final day of classes, anyway, and one more won't hurt. Next week is the study vac, when we're supposed to be fully involved in exam preparation. There'll be plenty of time to sleep after the exams, I reckon.

School sucks, but if I don't finish it, I can't get into uni. I want to study environmental science next year. Dad says they need young rangers in the national parks, and that'd be a cool job, but he says, about the only way to get it is if you have an environmental science certificate or a degree, these days. He says hundreds of people try out for ranger jobs every time they're advertised, so the competition is fierce, and if everyone else has a 'bit of paper', as he calls it, I'd have no chance without one. He thinks because I did two weeks seasonal work, fixing picnic tables in Kakadu last July, I might have an edge, but year 12 is still the first hurdle. The next will be to get my 'bit of paper'.

The November air is thick. It feels like you're drowning with each breath, but we've hardly had any rain yet. Every afternoon for weeks we look up at huge storm clouds that seem ready to burst, but they just float away over the horizon like Spanish galleons seeking their fortunes elsewhere. Everyone checks the "BOM Site" every day—the Bureau of Meteorology website is as popular as Google here.

As I lock the back door and go down the stairs, old Liquorice, our ancient black mongrel, flaps her tail against the cool concrete spot she likes under the laundry sink.

"Hello old girl," I say and scratch her ear. She stays there—the effort of moving around on this muggy morning is too much for her old bones. The sliding glass door of Charlie's granny flat is firmly closed and I wonder idly if he'll be back before my exams. Will he do the big brother thing and help me study? I doubt it, he's an electrician—and I am not doing any exams in anything he knows about. I don't need his help anyway.

Our garden is a jungle; big fan-leafed palms, tall Carpentaria palms and a range of ginger plants, spiky Pandanas, and several broad-leafed plants crowd the driveway on one side, so it's almost impossible to see into the neighbour's yard. A huge banyan tree dominates one of the back corners. When I was a kid, Dad tied a rope up on one of its branches and we used to swing on it for hours, but these days it is frayed and too weak to hold my weight. In the other corner, there's a magnificent mango tree. Now, and every November, its branches are dragged down by the weight of huge Kensington Prides. The fruit bats will soon come from miles around, as soon as night falls, to scrabble over ripe fruit, but there'll be enough to share. In the afternoons we'll also get magpie geese, sitting in the upper branches, honking and arguing amongst themselves. They always get the highest fruit.

Under the house, I skirt round the pile of empty boxes Dad and Mum have collected for the Great Mango Pick. Every year when the ripening fruit are showing their first tinge of yellow, Charles and I climb up and pick any we can reach and then we shake the branches to knock the others down. We fill up dozens of boxes and leave them for a while to ripen. Then there is a big family time of sitting round the table to dice them. Hundreds of them get sliced up and put in small bags for the freezer. That way we can have mango smoothies all year round. Mum makes a great mango ice-cream too. The Great Mango Pick must be soon—next time Charles is home, I guess.

As I leave the garden, I enter the bright sunlight in the street. After the shade of home, it's always a shock—the heat is intense. Actually, it's only about 34 degrees, but the direct sunlight seems much hotter because of the humidity. I don't mind, I like it, but I can feel the sweat on my back already. Like most people in Darwin, I am hanging out for the wet season to start.

The last few days of school have been a whirl of classes which produced an endless list of things I haven't learned, and have no recollection of them even being taught, so it's catch-up time. The smart kids in the front row seem to know everything already, but they always do. We call them the brainiacs. My mate Ben and I sit further back in class. Ben's been my mate forever and we hang out at recess and lunch every day.

Some of our subjects are the same. He's a keen skateboarder and wins competitions. After school and on weekends he'll usually be down at the Jingili Water Gardens skate-park and I sometimes ride my bike down there to watch him practice. He's studying for exams too, but doesn't have any plans for next year yet, except to go surfing. He says he's really good at that. He's going to Bali for the surf in Schoolies week, when the exams are over. He wants me to go too, but I can't surf to save my life.

2.

The first two exams seemed okay. It hasn't been such a bad experience. If I get a good enough ATAR I can get into University, but I have had to study to do that. I have no idea if I did enough, though, but my school marks so far are fine … well, maybe. Anyway, it'll all be over on Wednesday.

I put my brooms back in the storeroom. I have this job sweeping the laundry floor and the stairs of a block of flats in Coconut Grove. I've kept it going during the exam time for the money. It's shitty work, like the other day when I had to hose vomit off the steps. But the pay is above award wages and I've saved enough to pay for a Honda motorbike I am buying on Thursday, the day after the biology exam. I would have bought it weeks ago, but Dad won't let me until school is over. He reckons I'll end up with my leg in plaster, or a broken neck or something, and says the risk of riding a motorbike is too great and it's really hard doing exams in pain and plaster.

"Erasmus," he says, "these exams are the most important tests of your life. Good marks will open doors you can't even imagine yet, motorbikes can wait … You can go to hospital after you finish." And on and on he goes, but he's right, I guess. Anyway, it's given me a chance to save more money.

I look at my phone. Three thirty. Chemistry is tomorrow. I better get home and do some more study. My shirt is glued to my back and dark with sweat. Storm clouds are teasing the city in the distance.

My bicycle leans against the grey-brick yard that holds the wheelie bins out the front of the flats. Someone has cleaned some fish and dumped the heads and guts in one of the bins. The smell has gotten worse in the hour I've been working, and the flies have come from far and wide. I can hear them before I can see them. I ride away with the stench of rotting fish in my nostrils—an ocean warzone smell of death that follows me down the road. It's depressing. I decide for the hundredth time that I am going to quit this job as soon as I get the Honda.

I do most of my study on a small desk in my bedroom. It's up against the window and I look down to the pool. Sometimes the temptation is too much and I take my books down there and sit in the water to study. Distractions are easy to find. I've just sat down on the step when Ben calls me to ask about oxidation reactions. It's the blind leading the blind a bit, and I tell him so, but he says he's only started revising today, so any help he can get will be good.

We talk about chemistry for a while and then about surfing.

"Ah mate," he says, "when you race down the front of a big wave and it curls above you into a tube ... what a rush!"

"You're still going to Bali on Friday?" I ask, knowing the answer.

"Of course, Uluwatu here I come. There's just this shitty chemistry to get out of the way ..."

We wish each other good luck and hang up. I'll see him tomorrow.

3.

"Don't forget! Check and check again. You have three hours, Honey. Use them all!"

"Yeah Mum," I say. "Do you have to say that every exam?"

"I just want you to do your best, Ras. If you walk out and remember something, you can't go back to change an answer, you know …"

Mum goes on a bit sometimes like Dad, but she's alright, mostly. I suppose she's worried I'll be on the dole, and still at home, when I'm twenty-five. She needn't be—once I've got the Honda, I am planning on getting out and about and get a cooler job.

The exam starts at nine. I can feel a few butterflies in my belly. Only two more of these and I am finished school for ever. Twelve long years, and the rest of my life just starting—it feels like I am in a countdown to a new beginning. I have studied. I really have! Especially last night, after an hour in the pool. It was a last-minute effort and it's not much, I know, but it's too late now for anything else.

I promise Mum I'll stay the whole time as she drops me off in the College's drive-through. Ben's already here. I go over and stand with him in the breezeway. He nags me again to go to Bali with him for Schoolies—but I am buying the bike on Thursday, and anyway, I can't surf. I keep telling him, no.

"Ah well" he says. "You ready for chem?"

"As much as ever. I reckon it'll be alright."

At twenty to, a teacher calls us in. "Leave your phones in your bags", he says loudly. "AND TURN THEM OFF", even louder.

He's tall, thin and old. He's a new one I've never seen before. Must be a relief teacher, I think. He almost shouts "DON'T TALK" to us as we go into the hall even though no one has said a word. I have to check the board near the door for the seating plan. It's in alphabetical order and the names are also split into subject areas. I look for Erasmus Stokes. I am in D11 and I head to the fourth row. We are all quiet and sitting still, but the teacher tells us to be quiet again anyway, to put our name stickers on the exam answer booklet and put the covers of our calculators on the floor. Then the teachers go up and down the rows deleting the memory on any calculator that has one.

From D11, I can see that the hall has 'G' lines of pale desks and plastic chairs stretching from one end to the other. Two desks are empty, the papers lying on them telling stories of dickheads who have missed their bus or were too slack to get out of bed. Wankers who have thrown it all away at the eleventh hour!

The old teacher reads out the rules of the exam. Most of us have heard it a few times already, plus it was the same at the trials, so we don't listen. Then it's eight fifty.

"START READING," he calls. "You have ten minutes."

Paper rustles across the hall like a gust of wind in autumn. Ben is in C2. He won't last long. Jess Manton is nearer me in C10. I can just see her paper. Now there's some luck, maybe I'll get some answers from her. Nearly next to Jess Manton must be good. She's the queen of the brainiacs, the smartest kid in the class. She's wearing perfume—it's light and wafty, like flowers, and cool, and just a little distracting.

Chemistry! Ten minutes reading. Three hours sitting, brain burning carbs, sprouting knowledge to impress some stranger in Adelaide, with a steaming coffee cup at hand, going through my answers one by one.

These three final hours are the clincher. FOCUS! I tap my forehead with my knuckles.

I notice the paper's quality: the spare-no-expense type because THIS IS SERIOUS! There's fifteen pages … that's five pages per hour … one every twelve minutes …

Magnesium oxide acts as a catalyst in the conversion of vegetable oil into biodiesel. Cool. Did Mister teach us that? Then I spot the graph question.

"YOU MAY START," says the invigilator. I can read graphs; I'll start with that.

The grey carpet is chequered. I see that all the table legs in my row are lined up in the same line of squares except one. An outlier … a maverick, ha, like me …

If you put a little sodium hydroxide into canola oil, you get carboxylate salts. Bugger, I have to draw its damn ion. I'll guess. Two hours to go. Two hours? Water—I must hydrate or my brain will get cloggy. I raise my hand and ask for water. The teacher goes to fetch a cup. He's craggy and stooped, like a marabou stork. Creepy. And he's an invigilator! Great word for what must be a boring job, but he clearly takes his job seriously. He should have a T-shirt with it written on. I wonder if Schwarzenegger has made a movie called 'Invigilator Man'. He returns and places the polystyrene cup on my desk. His hand is a claw, bony, with blue veins showing through thin, lose skin. I try not to look at it.

I sip my water, feeling virtuous. I had a good breakfast. Protein, not sugar. Mister will be impressed—he drummed into us some brain science, trying to get us in peak thinking condition for exams. Maybe there's something in it.

Hey, lactose has a nice structure—pretty. It's got double carbon rings and lots of oxygen. But what is it? Can't be a protein, it doesn't have nitrogen ... it must be a sugar. Tick! An easy mark.

I need a piss and put my hand up. The teacher appears at my elbow in less than a second, as if by magic, and I jump. Okay, he was just behind me, but there's something unusual about him ... Anyway, Invigilator Man lets me go to the little room. He's so old he knows about having to piss, I reckon. Inside, I do ten star-jumps and a few knee pumps to push some cleansing blood through my brain. Mister said that will remove carbon dioxide and free radicals. 'Up here for thinking', I tap my forehead with my knuckles again.

Peptides. Circle one. What's a peptide link? Black or blue? Blue, a guess!

More water. It might make a difference, an extra mark through thinking more clearly. This is a competition after all and one extra mark may get me into CDU by beating some dehydrated fool who didn't do star-jumps in the dunny.

Thirty minutes to go. I am not allowed to leave now anyway. Ben has long gone. Jess will get an A like usual. Her writing is too small, so she's been no help. I can't see any gaps on her paper like there are on mine, but I can see her writing is incredibly neat. Depressing. Her hair flashes gold in the light as she moves, and I enjoy that. One strand has worked lose from her braids and it hangs down across her cheek. Her perfume gives me images of flowers in springtime.

I am nearly finished anyway, one question to go ... what the hell? What's a k_c value?

There aren't many of us left, basically just Jess and me and a few other brainiacs like Jess, scattered among the rows. I've sat here the whole three hours and ten minutes because I promised Mum, even though I could really have walked out an hour ago. I willed extra marks onto my paper and I am feeling confident. What I would most like to do right now is run my fingers through Jess Manton's hair.

I've been busy. I can tell you how many strips there are in each window blind and I would recognise Invigilator Man's footsteps with my eyes closed and … That amuses me. Perhaps they'll arrest him and ask me down to the cop shop and make me listen to people walk by in a line-up. I'd pick him easy because he taps his left foot on the ground every step he takes: *step, taptap, step, step, taptap, step*. Invigilator Man would go down for cruelty to kids! He took three hours from me I'll never see again. Jeez—where do they get these old buggers from anyway?

It occurs to me that the reason I know his footsteps so well is that he's always hovering around me. Me? No, I watch him for a minute. He's watching Jess. It's true! Wherever he is in the room he's always looking over at her. Strange.

"PENS DOWN, STOP WRITING," calls Invigilator Man and suddenly he's standing over Jess. Too close. The other invigilators are collecting papers, but he's distracted by her.

"How'd you go?" he asks, leering at her, his eyes beady and unblinking, bird-like. She just shrugs.

Creepy, I think again.

Jess and I get up at the same time and our eyes meet. I grin and try to convey a sense of achievement; *I've just aced that test too, Baby*.

We file out of the hall. It is hot outside, but I suddenly shiver, as if Invigilator Man has stolen some of my core body temperature. But it's just the release of tension, or adrenalin or something; can't pin everything on the old man.

4.

"Hey Ras, how'd it go, ya mongrel?"

Ben lounges on the bench of the concrete picnic table the school installed because it is too heavy for kids to move, and we'd need a jack hammer to carve our names in it.

"Crap, I reckon. What about you?"

"Easy," he says. "But I didn't do Part B."

"Eh? That's half the marks, you stupid moron."

Ben shrugs. "Well, can't do much about it now. Wanna come to the mall? Got any money."

"Not likely," I reply. "I've gotta study for Biology tomorrow."

"Hey, check out the brainiacs," he points his chin. They are under the frangipani tree boasting about their exams. White flowers are scattered on the ground around them as if in homage. Jess,

Ivana, Trevor the Nerd and the Whinging Pom, and a few others, are all there.

"Look at them," I say, "The school's royalty. Them-That-Can-Do-No-Wrong!" It's true—everyone knows they're the kids who'll be getting ninety-five plus for their ATARs. Jess's golden hair flashes in a ray of sunshine.

Ben thinks I crush on Jess. Most blokes do, I reckon, and he would too, but as far as he knows she doesn't surf, so in his view there's no point in being interested. She's the hottest girl in school and way out of my league, I think. I have never even spoken to her. He chuckles and saunters off to pick up his skateboard. I watch the brainiacs for a while. For most of year 12, my mates had either regarded them with awe and envy, or loathing and distaste, depending on any looming due dates for assignments. They have it easy. They listen to the teacher, understand what is said and then regurgitate on command. Just like that! It sucks! I thought of biology. They wouldn't be worried, a walk in the park. I turn to start the walk home.

"Hi."

It's Jess, all smiles and sunshine.

"How was it?"

"B-Brilliant," I swallow. "Easy, no worries." Wow!

"Great," she says. Her soft dark brown eyes gaze at me. "You were working the whole time … you surprised me."

"Ah well, I studied a lot." I say. "These exams are pretty important. How about you?"

"For days and days and Dad got me a tutor who really helped. Chemistry is really hard."

Oh, I think. Who knew that brainiacs had to study hard?

"Ah," I say.

Jess looks up at me again. The tip of her tongue appears briefly in the corner of her mouth.

"It's good to be finished. Anyway, um, I was thinking," she says. Is she blushing? "Do you want to come to the mall with me? You know, hang out?"

"Sure," I say. "It's only biol tomorrow, my last one. No worries, I got that in the bag. How 'bout you?"

"I'm done," she said. "I'm free."

She gazes off into the distance, lost in her thoughts. I study her closely. God, she's beautiful. I've never really been this close to her before—she's always surrounded by the other brainiacs. I spent most of the year watching the back of her head from three rows behind. Reluctantly, I have to admit to myself that Ben is right, I do have a crush on her. She frowns and a small line briefly appears between her eyebrows. Then it's gone …

"What's wrong?" I ask.

"Nothing … it's just that, you know, that's it. It's all over. No more school! It seems a bit of an anticlimax."

"Yeah, know what you mean," I said, not having a clue. "It's a bit weird, hey?"

We walk slowly through the school. This is her last time in school uniform. As we pass the front of the hall, Invigilator Man comes out carrying the box of completed exams. He sees Jess and his face twists into a toothy grin and his eyes become mere points in his sagging features. Then he winks at her. Jess doesn't respond— maybe that's what girls have to put up with all the time, I think, but it's a bit much coming from a teacher.

We move out from the under-croft but are beaten back by the heat of the asphalt, so we skirt the carpark until we get in the shade of the jacaranda trees, still dropping their red petals across the ground.

Hey look at me! I am walking into the Logies, across a red carpet, escorting a famous actress. I look at Jess. The black and mauve school uniform spoils the effect a little, I vaguely wonder what she'd wear if it really was a red carpet. My uniform is doomed—I'm planning to burn it on Wednesday.

"When's your plane?" she asks.

"Hey, mate!" It was Ben. "Where're you going? Thought you were gunna study."

He is on his skateboard—a big one, half his height. He always says it's like surfing to school when he uses his big board, takes his mind off things. I mumble something to him, but he doesn't listen, Neanderthal way—the communication of good mates. What plane? I wonder. Ben cruises on, chuckling to himself.

It's hot. Gee, we need rain … We walk in silence for a while—I concentrate when crossing Bagot Road as there's cars everywhere and I don't want Jess in danger—then, on the footpath, I walk behind her so that the kids on bikes can get past without hitting her and I can watch the light in her hair. We duck through the petrol station, fall into the shade of the carpark, then cut through the cars to get to the entrance of the mall.

Casuarina Square sure has changed a lot recently. There's a whole new outdoor section full of restaurants under the cinema and a water garden where little kids play next to the Baskin-Robbins ice-cream shop. I stop there.

"Want an ice-cream?"

"Not really," she says. "Let's get a smoothie, and we can sit over there in the aircon that comes out of the mall. School is over, I want to do different things now."

I pay. Can't get my wallet out fast enough. She thanks me quietly. We sit on the black concrete walls at the front of one of the new shops. A cool breeze of electric air blows from inside every time someone walks through the automatic door. I wonder how her eyes can be dark brown then light brown, then hazel, then flecked with gold all in about five seconds.

The loose strand of blonde hair is sticking to Jess's cheek. Horses sweat, men perspire and ladies merely glow, I can hear mum saying. Well, after the hot walk from the college I am a horse, but Jess sure glows.

She runs a finger around her ear and the loose strand whips away behind it. I feel a moment of loss and an urge to pull it back.

"I can't wait till we're there. It's going to be such fun. The exchange rate is really good at the moment.

Exchange rate?

"Er …"

"Where are you staying? We'll be at the Agung. My Grandmother is Indonesian, we go to Java to visit her a lot. In Bali we usually stay at the

Agung with Mum and Dad? Do you know it?"

"No."

"It's easy to find. On Jalan Legian. This is going to be so cool—I've never been there without my parents before. No more school, we're free. Schoolies week will be the best."

The penny drops. Aha! Schoolies! She's going to Bali. I had told Ben no, why spend all that money? An image of my Honda flashes in front of me. A whole year's work sweeping those stupid stairs to get it! But for some reason Jess thinks I'll be in Bali, like her. I am about to tell her I have other plans, but she goes on:

"I get there on Wednesday night, at ten o'clock. Then the party starts." She sucks on her smoothie for a second and gazes deeply into my eyes. "It'll be really cool to hang out there with my friends. When did you say you'll be there?"

I can hear my blood pumping. Friends! Wow, I have unfamiliar feelings. Is this our first date, I wonder?

"Friday night," I say, convincingly. "I've never been there before. This will be my first trip."

Yes, Friday. I'll join Ben. Better call him and find out more. I am going to have to splash out after all. I can sweep more steps for the Honda when I come back!

"Great," she says. "I can show you around."

"Can't wait," I say. We smile. Her eyes change colour again. Really!

5.

I call Ben's mobile.

"Hey, I have decided to come with you on Friday. You reckon I'll still get a ticket?"

"You can try. Great, what's brought about this change?" he asks.

"I'll tell you later. Are you home? I'm coming over—get online and see if there's any seats."

By the time I arrive at Ben's place he's looked up Air Asia and the website says, "Less than 5 seats left." We make a booking using Ben's mum's credit card. I will pay her back tomorrow, I promise her. Phew. It's all go, now.

Then I rush off to do my cleaning job. When I get home, I tell Dad and Mum the news.

"You what?" Dad is astonished. "You've never mentioned Bali before. I thought you were saving for the bike."

"Yeah, I am … was. They'll hold it for me … or find another buyer. I'm only going for six days—I can go back to work when I get back." Visions come to me of a future of stinking fish guts and dirty, vomit-stained stairwells—I hope it's worth it, I think.

Dad doesn't like surprises very much, he complains about me going off half-cocked and being unreliable, not following through on promises. I have never shown any interest in surfing before, he says. In the end, however, as Mum tells him, I am, after all, eighteen years old and it's my money. I haven't told either of them about Jess.

"He's old enough to vote," she says. "So, he's old enough to spend his money the way he wants. And he's studied so hard for his exams."

Dad calmed down but looked a bit sulky. "I just think people need to do what they say they're going to do, not rush off half-cocked on a whim …"

I nearly ask them what they have done with my real mum and dad. They wouldn't have agreed so easily a year ago. But come to think of it, both Mum and Dad have been treating me differently the last few months. As exams approached and they could see me studying, I guess they were letting go a bit. Is this what growing up means, I wonder?

I feel a little pang of guilt. Maybe I should have studied more rather than playing with my phone, or secetly reading those Barry Jonsberg novels hidden inside my textbooks, when they were around, so they'd think I was hard at it. But it's dark now and I still have one more exam tomorrow. I will have to do my usual last-minute cram. I have probably left it too late, but I have always liked biology, so I know most of it anyway.

6.

I think I have had enough sleep, but I am too excited about Bali and Jess to think much of anything else. The exam is a blur that comes and goes, but I reckon I got through it alright. After it's over some of us head to the biology lab and eat a cake one of the girls brought in to say thanks to the teacher because she was the best. Jess will be in Bali tonight, with her mates. I still have two days to wait.

Even with the cake, the end of school is all a bit of an anti-climax, like it was for Jess the other day. Now I understand what she meant. I mean, is that really it? No more school? The biology teacher is upbeat. She always has a little song or a rhyme for everything, so, as usual, when she recites a poem that must have come from the nineteen twenties, no one is surprised:

No more Latin,
No more French,
No more sitting on a hard board
bench.
No more rulers,
No more books,
No more teachers' dirty looks.

And we all groan and grin with the agony of it.

And in two days I'll be in Bali. I can see Jess waiting at the airport, a flower in her hair, running into my arms as I come out. "Oh Ras," she will say, breathlessly, "I thought you'd never get here." And we'll find some coconut-leaf bungalow on a deserted island beach and go skinny dipping in a crystal-clear lagoon, and drink coconut milk and massage each other with sweetly scented oil …

At home, I don't actually burn my uniform, like I'd planned to for the last six months, because Mum gets me to put all my school clothes in a bag for the op-shop. Some other sucker will wear them.

Ben calls. He's on task and is planning to take two boards. He asks me if I will call one a part of my luggage to save him money. I drop round to his house, because it's no problem, and I help him pack them up. Ben has already had two days of post-school freedom. It's strange but when I look at him, he already seems more relaxed. His hair looks longer, the singlet he is wearing is a bit cooler than before and the down that was on his face is now looking more like a beard than fluff. Amazing.

I do my own packing at home and remember to ask Dad to get my passport from where it's locked in his desk drawer. I go to the bank for some cash to pay Ben's mum back and get a wad of crisp new fifty-dollar notes for spending money. I look at my bank balance and sigh—and think goodbye to the Honda—at least for a while.

In the evening, Mum and Dad want to come to the airport and say goodbye, but I convince them not to.

"It's only for a few days and I am not a school kid anymore," I say. Dad laughs that irritating dad-laugh he has that suggests he knows better, but ...

"Just remember your manners," he said for the ten thousandth time. "There's no excuse for bad manners anywhere, anytime ..."

"... or with anybody," Mum and I say together to finish his mantra. Dad really believes this. He's the politest man you'll ever meet.

Ben's Mum drops us both off outside the airport door and drives away with a wave and we check in together—two cool international surfer dudes.

We have to take the surfboards down to the oversized luggage area, but nothing is too much trouble and it makes me feel like a surfer too. We're both excited. We are due to arrive at ten. Ben knows a cheap hotel called Taman Sari, where he's stayed before, on Poppies Lane, and says we'll get there by taxi before eleven, then go out. I say that that's exactly what I want to do— I'll be able to meet Jess.

Then an announcement over the airport PA. Due to 'technical difficulties' and the late arrival of the plane, we will be delayed. Bugger!

I buy some rupiah at a lousy exchange rate at a kiosk, while we are waiting, just to fill in time, and the evening drags on. We have nothing else to do but sit and wait. A few other kids from my school are scattered among the crowd. I know some of them and they know me, but the delay is a real downer and no one is feeling sociable. A couple of blokes are playing cards but mostly we ignore each other in stoic resilience. When at last we board the plane, we are three hours late and already half asleep. Ben and I doze, on and off, most of the way.

In Bali we are off the plane quickly because our seats were near the front. We are hit by the warm, damp Bali air as we climb down the stairs and get directed to a red and white Air Asia bus that's parked in front of the plane. When we get on, I go to sit down but Ben makes me stand next to the doors on the other side of the plane. It's a good move, because we're off first when the bus stops to let us off. The airport is huge. There's a lot of people heading towards the passport control and Ben makes me walk fast to get in front of some of them. He's been here before, so I do as I am told—respecting his expertise. There's a million people lined up at immigration. I groan—this is going to take a long time. I stop at the closest line, but Ben tugs my backpack.

"Follow me" he says.

There are four lines zigzagging into the check points and Ben has spotted one he likes more. It seems the same length to me.

"Look closely," he says, with his patient look on, like he's tutoring maths. "There's a big difference. Your line has a package tour in it from China or somewhere. They all know each other; see how they're standing closer together."

He was right, there was double the number of people in the same area. "That line will be slow," he says.

"And that line there," he is pointing. "Look at the immigration counters—there is only one officer working. We have two. Trust me, this line will be quicker."

He's right, it still takes ages, but we're through long before many other people on the plane. It all evens out though, because we get to the luggage carousel and have to wait. No luggage appears for another half hour and it takes another twenty minutes to collect the surfboards and our bags— we almost convince ourselves that they were lost.

Then we have to put everything through x-ray machines at Customs. We line up for that too, before walking through a metal detector. A customs officer asks to check one of my bags. For no reason I feel nervous, but he just has a quick look, then waves me through.

We pay for a taxi at the airport taxi counter. There are dozens of Balinese men who try and get us to employ them. "Taxi, taxi. Where are you going?" we're asked over and over, but Ben just pushes through them without speaking. I follow. One bloke is particularly insistent, and even though we're following an official driver we've already paid, he keeps asking.

"Where you go?"

I am tired. It's been a long night already.

"Piss off," I shout at him and walk faster. Annoying prick!

The only advantage of arriving in the small hours of the morning is there is no traffic. The taxi ride is quick because most of the streets are empty, the shops have their metal roller doors firmly padlocked and mangy dogs prowl around, looking for discarded food in the piles of rubbish left on the street for the early morning collectors. Dad warned me before we left that some Balinese dogs have rabies, so we should be careful of them.

Dazed, we finally arrive at the hotel about three in the morning—dead tired. I am in a foul mood, but Ben is more fatalistic about the delay. He has been here many times and has a good-natured shrug-the-shoulders attitude, but I hate it. Not a good start, I think.

7.

It's about ten—bright shards of light slash through cracks in the doors and shutters, adding happiness in skinny spotlights on the beds and walls, whilst keeping most of the room gloomy. It's not too early to go out and I feel better now. Sleep is a great tonic. I stretch luxuriously on the bed, under my single sheet. No need for blankets here, just like home. A ceiling fan clucked away as it spun above us during the night to keep us cool. Ben is asleep, or in a coma, I dunno, he was pretty buggered when we got in. Me too—our plan of hitting the town had collapsed, and we did too. But now I am ready to greet the world. This is my first time in Bali—six days of fun in the party town of Kuta.

Everything here is weird—like the narrow, carved doors that open onto our balcony. They open in the middle and I have to use both. I know I can't fit through just one because I was jammed between them last night, for a second. They don't even have proper doorhandles, just hanging rings that swing freely, and they're locked by a sliding wooden bar on the inside, or a small padlock on the outside.

I am ready to open both the doors and start the day by ducking out and buying some bottled water, but as I open the door, I hear a couple of people about to pass our room. I pause to let them by. I don't want to make too much noise or crowd the narrow balcony outside. They walk past; *step, taptap, step, step, taptap, step* ...

I forgot my wallet and go back to pick it up, then put on my thongs, open the doors and enter the day, leaving Ben to his slumber. Downstairs the pool looks really nice, but the smell of chlorine is strong. It was dark last time I saw it, but a sign that said "No Swimming after 10pm" was well lit. There are two pools, a small wading pool for kids and a big deep pool. The water is blue and inviting. I am looking forward to having a swim, later.

A couple of Hindu statues stand along the back wall. To the left are shade umbrellas and sun lounges, but the other side runs directly into the restaurant. A careless diner could move their chair back on the tiles and tip into the water. Some of the bushes in the garden are growing in white concrete pots and their leaves are cut in the shape of balls, like globes of the earth on sticks, or huge green lollipops. Everything is neat. A low white wall separates the pool from the path. The hotel reception is across the path from the restaurant and there's a wooden door between them that leads to the street. I move towards the door. Two guests are sitting in the restaurant ordering their breakfasts. I recognise one of them immediately.

Shiiit! I pull quickly behind a pillar. It's Invigilator Man!

What the hell? What's he doing here? I don't want him to see me. Where can I go? He's sitting at a table right next to the circular stairs facing the door. I have to walk past him to get out onto Poppies Lane. I can see a lot of people passing by outside and hear a constant low roar of motorbikes. Invigilator Man is here! And in my way! I duck down behind the wall.

A waitress smiles at me.

"Selamat pagi," she sings. Shhh, I mime, finger to my lips. I wave her away and press close to the white painted bricks of the wall. I can smell concrete.

Invigilator Man is drinking coffee—his boney fingers twisting awkwardly to hold the tiny cup. He is wearing a white T-shirt that drapes down from his thin shoulders like a curtain. A row of bumps down the centre of his back marks his vertebrae. His pale arms are thin and hairy. If he held them wide, they would extend from his shirt like the stick arms of a skinny snow man. He is hunched, head forward, looking like one of those vultures that sit around in Western movies, waiting for someone to die. He is talking to a red-faced man with a huge belly and a walrus moustache. The contrast is amusing, but I would rather not see it. He doesn't see me because he's half facing away.

I decide I am being silly—maybe he won't recognise me anyway. I am not listening to what he is saying. I am planning my escape; all I hear is:

"...mumble mumble mumble mumble mumble mumble mumble mumble mumble mumble mumble mumble sex mumble mumble mumble ..."

What? Sex? He's talking about sex. I lean closer to listen.

" ...and Jess will do what I say!" he says.

Jess?

I peek around the pillar. He's showing Redface a picture on his phone.

"Here she is," he says.

"Yeah pretty ... eighteen already, you say? Gee they grow up quick ..." says Redface.

Invigilator Man holds his phone up and squints at the photo. I can see it too. It's Jess, smiling, looking lovely in a red bikini. Invigilator Man has a picture of *my girl* on his phone in a red bikini! A blue vein pulses in the crinkled skin of his neck. The creep!

"Gorgeous!" he says, "I'll find her later."

Bloody hell! I have to warn her. I have heard about these old blokes. They come to Bali looking for young girls and spike their drinks and ... *Shit*! He's been planning this since the exam! I knew there was something weird about him. There must be a word for this type of man.

They are getting up, paying for their coffee, going out. I follow. Ha! They went the wrong way, The Agung is on Legian, and I know that's left out of Poppies, and a few hundred meters from the corner on the right-hand side, because I looked it up on Google when I was at home.

I have a quick look at the shops nearby and duck into an Alpha-Mart for some water. There's a cool looking DVD shop next door I'll have to check out later—movies only cost one dollar, amazing, and beside that there is a 5D cinema. That'll be cool too! But for now, I have to warn Jess. I set off for the Agung.

8.

"Selamat pagi," I say to the Indonesian bloke in reception.

"G'day mate," he replies. I am not yet used to Indonesians picking me out as an Aussie. Must be my Darwin thongs ... I had maybe twenty blokes saying *g'day* to me, in fake Aussie accents, as I walked down Legian: "G'day mate, transport?" ... "G'day mate, girl?" ..."G'day mate, hash?"

"Piss off," I said to them. It was only half past ten!

The Agung is a bungalow hotel with a narrow, gated entrance. It has lots of two-story buildings scattered around the gardens and a huge lake swimming pool in the middle. The bloke at reception says he doesn't know Jess Manton, but I don't believe him.

" …you know," I say. "Really pretty, blonde hair, brown eyes …?"

"Yes," says the man. "We have many like that."

He won't let me in to look around. Against hotel policy he says. He's getting agitated and I reckon he'll kick me out soon.

But then: "Hello, stranger …"

It's Jess! I turn to find her behind me. She's wearing a sarong tied to her waist and a red bikini top. Her skin is tanned honey-brown and wet, she's just been swimming. Her hair is tied up on her head and dry. A strand of loose hair hangs down across her cheek, demanding attention. A thin silver armband runs around her upper arm. She has a pink frangipani flower tucked above her perfect ear. For a moment I can't speak …

She smiles with her eyes. Does she know the effect she's having on me? I blush.

"H-How you going?" I say. I catch her scent—flowers wafting on the breeze.

"Great. We looked for you at Sky Garden last night, did you go?"

"No, the plane was late, we just went to sleep. We're staying in a little place just down the road, in Poppies Lane."

"Cool," she says. "Have you had breakfast?"

I shake my head. She smiles her perfect teeth

at the reception man. "I have a guest, Gusti." He manages a nod. We go through to the buffet.

I take a tour of the groaning tables of the hotel's smorgasbord and choose a banana pancake to start with. Jess is already eating melon and pawpaw when I get to the table and a uniformed waiter, in Balinese head gear, is pouring her a coffee. She has chosen a six-seater table which overlooks the pool. Some kids are splashing in it at the other end, below a huge statue of a Balinese god pouring water out of a pot into the pool. Other guests are coming in for breakfast and the tables are filling up around us.

I need to tell her about Invigilator Man, but how? I don't want to sound like an idiot.

"Jess, I have something to …"

"Good morning, Jessy." It's Ivana and Trevor the Nerd, holding hands. I didn't know they were together. "Sleep well?"

They nod 'hi' to me and sit down. "Where's Lou?"

"She's still asleep," says Jess. "No, there she is."

The Whinging Pom slumps into a chair. "I feel ill," she says in her accent. "I ate something that disagrees with me."

My mates call Louise "The Whinging Pom" not because she comes from England, but because she once complained about the English class getting an extension on the due date for an assignment. We all thought that was just about the strangest thing anyone would ever do.

"Oh, poor darling. Do you still want to go to Water Bom Park?" asked Jess.

"No," says Lou. "I'm going back to bed."

Jess frowns, that little fold between her eyebrows appears. She looks at me. The tip of her tongue appears briefly in the corner of her mouth. "Hey, I know. Ras, do you want to come to Water Bom Park with us today?"

I am looking at her eyebrows, dreaming, but I suddenly realise she is talking to me. I must look startled.

"Um, sure, yes," I say. She smiles at me. I push aside thoughts of Invigilator Man. No doubt I imagined it all, anyway.

Ivana and Trevor are gazing into each other's eyes—not such nerds after all.

9.

We are sitting outside Starbucks having iced tea and sticky cinnamon buns. I reckon we went on every ride in the park, because Jess wanted to try them all. I am exhausted. It was an expensive day. Water Bom Park was really crowded—if everyone spent as much money as we did the owners must have gold plated taps at home. Jess sucks on her straw. She is more radiant and alive than anyone I've ever seen before. Ivana and Trevor have gone into the mall, shopping.

"You know," she says, pulling stray hair back over her ear, "all those scary drops and rides are okay I guess, but my favourite was the Lazy River."

"Me too," I reply, but only because we shared a double float and Jess sat in the first ring, between my knees and held onto my toes in the rapids. "It was a good laugh." We were hopeless sailors and kept spinning round in the current—our raft seemed to have a mind of its own and wanted to travel backwards. We were hysterical with laughter at one point. Little kids around us must have thought we were crazy.

As we had left the park, I had seen the sign for Starbucks in Discovery Mall across the road and we had climbed up the huge set of stairs to get to it. Jess asked to sit outside because the air conditioning inside was too cold.

I look around at the shops and the hundreds of tourists and Indonesians everywhere. Starbucks is nestled between Pizza Hut and the mall entrance, and there's a KFC a little way away. "We could be anywhere in the world", I say.

"Yeah," says Jess. "Except Darwin."

We relax under a green umbrella and watch the world go by. I remember I was going to warn her about Invigilator Man. Even if I was imagining it, there's no harm in giving her the heads-up. I prepare myself, working out what to say.

"Jess ..." but she asks me what time we should go out tonight.

"I dunno, what do you think?"

"Come to the Agung at nine," she says, watching me carefully. The tip of her tongue appears briefly in the corner of her mouth.

Any time you say, I think.

"Okay" I say. And then I think: I don't have to tell her about the danger she's in after all. She'll be all right if I am with her. And suddenly I have a plan. I can protect her. If Invigilator Man tries something, I can drive him off. I'd be Jess's hero.

We put our cups in the bin and climb down the stairs to a Bluebird taxi. Jess tells the driver where to go, in fluent Indonesian, and he muscles his car through the Bali traffic back to Legian.

We have to go the long way round Kuta because of the one-way road system and we get really comfortable in the taxi, almost dozy. I lose my concentration. The taxi stops outside the Agung and I pay the fare. Jess is already climbing out the door on the left side, but suddenly I see Invigilator Man walking out the gates of the hotel. Shiiit! I panic. Without thinking I grab Jess's waist and roughly pull her back in the car. She's startled.

"What the … Ras …?" she starts. I think fast.

"Um.., let's go to the movies," I say. "Right now."

"Ras, I am tired. I want to rest, what are you doing?" I am looking around wildly. I have lost sight of Invigilator Man. No, there he is. He's walking away. Phew, he didn't see us.

My heart is pumping so loud, I think Jess must be able to hear it.

"Err … nothing," I say. "I just thought it would be a good idea."

She's annoyed, I can see. Some hero I am! The traffic has banked up behind us and drivers are now blowing their horns. "You're being weird, Ras."

"Sorry," I say. "Maybe tomorrow, hey?"

Jess climbs out of the car and starts walking towards the Agung. I scramble out after her, but it's okay now. Invigilator Man is fifty meters away telling a motorbike guy that no, he doesn't want transport.

"See you at nine?" I call after her. She stops and turns and looks at me. She doesn't say anything for a while. Her eyes are dark and there's a line between her eyebrows. But then she seems to soften. She's made up her mind, the line disappears.

"Okay, 9 o'clock. Don't be late" she flashes a small smile, then spins around and goes through the hotel gate. Phew, that was close, I think. I nearly blew it.

I hang around outside the Agung, just in case Invigilator Man comes back, but I am beginning to feel stupid. I decide he is long gone. I start back to my hotel to look for Ben.

10.

"Who?" asks Ben.

"From the chemistry exam ... the invigilator. You remember him? Tall, old bloke, funny walk."

"Nah, I dunno who you're talking about. I wouldn't know any of those teachers again."

"Well, he's staying here. In this hotel."

"He's probably on holiday. D'you reckon he's a surfer?"

"No, you don't understand. He's a creep. I saw him showing another old bloke a photo of Jess on his phone. And then I saw him coming out of Jess's hotel. I think he's stalking her ... she's in danger, Ben."

"Ah, come on Ras, that doesn't seem very likely. Why would he follow her to Bali?"

"Because she's got no one to look after her here," I reply.

Except me, I think.

Ben is clearly unconvinced. He's off surfing tomorrow with some new mates he met on the waves in Uluwatu, so he's got other things to think about. He isn't even going out with us tonight because they're picking him up before dawn tomorrow.

I sneak downstairs to see if Invigilator Man is in the restaurant. It's getting dark now, but there's no sign of him. I am standing partly hidden by a pot plant with blue berries hanging from its branches, but I have a good view—he's definitely not there.

"Excuse me."

I am startled. Redface has appeared suddenly behind me and is pushing past me, sideways, on the path. His belly is so big, it is hard for him to fit through the gap. I must have looked really jumpy or something, because he looks at me curiously for a moment. Until I say, "Sorry Mate," and pull back off the path. Redface moves into the restaurant. I feel embarrassed and turn quickly to go back to my room. I nearly walk right into Invigilator Man. He towers over me, like a huge stooped crane.

"Careful there, Sonny," he says, "what's the hurry?"

"Um, er, sorry," I say and sidestep around

him. He didn't recognise me! I scarper back to the room. My heart is pounding. I sit on the bed to think.

"What's up?" asks Ben. "You look like you've seen a ghost."

"I just met Invigilator Man. I don't think he recognised me."

"Well, why should he? There were hundreds of kids in the exams. There's nothing special about you, you know."

Maybe Ben is right. It's not as if he did anything for me, other than fetch water. I was just one of the crowd and not a pretty girl, like Jess.

"People only remember people who are beautiful, or ugly, not the average," Ben says. He's probably right. "On second thoughts," he continues, "on those grounds, there's no reason he'd forget a mug like yours."

"Ha ha," I reply.

I have about an hour and a half before meeting Jess. I figure it would be a good investment in time to have a nap before going out, so I lie on my bed and stare at the ceiling.

11.

"Hey Ras, aren't you going out tonight?"

Ben's voice enters my dream.

"Ra-as, it's nine-fiftee-een ..." he sings.

What? I spring out of bed, instantly awake. "What? Why didn't you wake me? Shit. I am late."

Shit! No time to shower. I change my T-shirt and grab my wallet and leave the hotel at a run. It's only five minutes, but I am in Legian, and nearly at the Agung, when I hear my name.

"Ras!"

It's Jess. She, Lou, Ivana and Trevor are walking along the path on the other side of the road. I cross to join them, panting and dripping with sweat.

"You're late," says Jess. "We gave up waiting for you."

"Sorry, I was delayed," I say. Then I grin and try to look cute. "Better late than never?"

"Maybe." Jess is cool towards me. That's twice I've annoyed her! She continues walking.

"Where are we going?" I ask.

"Sky Garden first, they have a 'Schoolies' party," says Lou, enthusiastically. "Then we're heading back to Paddy's, maybe Apache, Kudeta … I hope you're a good dancer, Ras …" she giggles.

Dance? Bugger! I hadn't thought of that. A girl I know once said I dance like Mr Bean. Not cool. I am worried now. What will Jess think of that? Geez! Why is life so hard?

We walk along Legian, ignoring the touts who are still saying "g'day mate, change-money?", "hash-hash?", "massage?" or "where you going, Boss? transport". I walk behind the others, shy of being too close to Jess—I sense she is still mad at me, and anyway, I am still sweating from my run. I must smell like a gym.

Walking behind her, I can see the effect Jess has on the locals, and the tourists, as she walks along. Men gawk at her. Women observe her carefully. She's beautiful all right. But she doesn't notice them and seems to enjoy looking in the windows of the big sports shops we pass.

We arrive at Sky Garden. Pretty black-eyed Indonesian girls, in red mini-dresses and platform shoes, smile and flirt and encourage people to go inside. We push through the crowd. There are lots of happy Schoolies from Australia, plus heaps of other tourists and back packers from all over the world. We have to pay an entry fee, which isn't cheap, but we get two paper tokens for drinks with it. Security guards check the girls' bags and Jess leads us upstairs. A waiter, with a very cool bleached-blonde haircut, guides us to a table. It is very loud, but early, and the crowd is still coming in. Music is pumping from huge speakers and 'DJ Komes', behind his board, clearly likes to extend his vowel sounds out for long seconds: "Welcome to Bal-eeeeeeee" he shouts, "Tonight is the night for danciiiiiiiiiiiiing" and people shout, and about fifty of them are on the dance floor already, as the beat of the music goes faster. Justin Bieber! Give me strength, I think to myself.

The waiter is asking what we'd like to drink. I can't hear what the others are ordering, but I ask for a Bintang. He disappears into the crowd to get the drinks. Ivana and Trevor join the dancers and Jess, Lou and I sit at the table watching them, unable to talk with the noise. I don't know what to do, so do nothing. Should I ask Jess to dance? Visions come to me of Mr Bean and suddenly I am shy.

The drinks arrive. The others have glass jars with handles—vodka cocktails, I guess. Cool. My Bintang beer is cold and wet but looks cheap and ordinary beside them.

Lou shouts something into Jess's ear and she nods. They get up. Jess looks at me briefly. But then she points to her handbag, then me. I nod. She smiles and follows Lou, and they push through to the dance floor. I faithfully guard the handbags and the drinks, aware that I can't leave them, in case someone steals them, or drops something into them. I drink my beer, watching Jess's body move, when I can catch a glimpse of her through the crowd. I wave my empty bottle at a waiter and he brings me a fresh one—and the second drink for the others, without being asked, and takes all the drink tokens as payment. By my third beer I have to pay cash. I can't hear how much I need, so just hand over a bunch of notes and, after a while, he brings the beer with some change, though I don't count it.

Jess and Lou are both great dancers, but I start to see less of them, from the table, as the crowd gets thicker.

They dance for ages. I feel alone and miserable. Some bloke comes by and offers to sell me a tablet of ecstasy. I tell him to piss off. I sip some of the vodka from Trevor's jar. Just a taste. It's sweet and strong. Then I sip some from Ivana's. Then I feel guilty and drink the same amount from both Jess's and Lou's jars, so that their levels are the same. I think they won't notice when they come back from the dancefloor. I spend a while making sure all their levels are the same, then remember that the girls had already sipped on theirs, but Trevor and Ivana hadn't. I take a little more out of Jess's and Lou's drink to hide my error.

Trevor comes back. He mouths: "Is this mine?" and I nod. He picks the jar up and sips the liquor. It is a third empty, but he doesn't notice and he takes it back to the dance floor and dances with it. I see the girls dancing together. Then they come back, breathless. Jess picks up her jar and holds it level to her eye. It's half empty. That little line between her eyebrows appears briefly. She looks at me and the tip of her tongue again appears briefly in the corner of her mouth. I feel giddy and just grin back at her. Within a few minutes, they've all started on their second drink. I realise that I have already drunk a lot of their first drinks, plus my three beers, and haven't yet had a dance.

The crowd is now huge and the girls want to move on, away from the crush of Sky Garden. Jess doesn't want to finish her drink and hands it to me and I skull it. When we get up to go outside, I feel a bit unsteady on my feet, but I am ready for the next adventure.

"How about some reggae?" asks Trevor, and he and Ivana are off straight away down the alley into Apache, from which we can hear a Bob Marley song blasting. We follow them, me grinning broadly. More drinks. This time I say I want a vodka cruiser—wow, it's strong. Ivana and Jess disappear to the ladies. Lou asks me if I want to dance and before I can answer, drags me onto the floor. The reggae beat is easy to dance to, even when carrying a bottle of vodka cruiser and I do a really good job. When I look back towards our table, I see Jess watching me. Maybe I am not such a bad dancer after all.

Jess comes onto the floor with Trevor and dances like an angel. Me too.

I try the twist but slip and land on the floor, but I am really fast in getting up, I am sure Jess doesn't notice. It's all skill. I haven't spilt a drop of my vodka. I have reactions like a steel trap. Lou notices, but just laughs.

"You all right?" she asks. "Better slow down on the vodka, Ras."

"All good here," I assure her and twirl into a ballet pirouette that must have looked awesome. I can't believe I was too shy to dance before. I am really good. I get wilder. Sweat flies from my forehead and drops onto the dance floor. I notice Lou has moved back to give me more room. The beat is mine. I own the floor. The whole crowd draws back in awe, to give me more space, and I swing my arms and kick my feet up. When the music stops, I think they might applaud, but no one does. I walk back to our table and drain my vodka all at once. God! I am hungry. I realise I haven't eaten anything since we were in Starbucks that afternoon, and that was just a cinnamon roll.

Jess says it's time to go and they start pushing through the crowd towards the exit. She's left half her drink behind. What a waste! I finish it off, and Lou's too, then hurry after her. They are standing in the street. I haven't danced with Jess yet, but with new confidence I am keen. We can go next door to Paddy's or the Bounty.

"Come on, Baby," I say, putting my arm around her waist. I will lead her to the dance floor and start to brush back the lose strand of blond hair that had fallen across her cheek.

But Jess twists out of my hold.

"No, Ras. It's time to go home."

"What? It's early, the night is a pup …"

"Go home Ras. We'll see you tomorrow." And at that they all turn round and start walking back to their hotel. Jess is angry. For what? I am speechless. I stand there with my mouth open. What went wrong?

Then a girl with a tray of cigarettes approaches me.

"Come inside Paddy's Bar," she says. "It's happy hour, all night." I look at the entrance. It has a huge gateway painted like a Disney castle and there are dozens of red, white and blue balloons forming an archway, and right next door is the Bounty. Maybe I should capitalise on my newfound dancing skills.

"Ok," I agree. "One more drink …"

12.

I wake slowly. Did I have an accident? Am I in hospital? I am sore all over; my head aches and I have the worst taste in my mouth. I roll over. The pillow is wet ... and it smells. I open my eyes. I have just rolled into vomit. Green vomit! I remember the huge green plastic cups of Long Island Tea I had drunk in the Bounty and have vague recollections of taking my shirt off and dancing up on stage in a bird cage and the girls chanting:

"Take it off. Take it off ..."

I suppose I must have had a good time, but right now my eyes hurt. I am in my room, but the bright strips of light slicing through the gaps in the shutters are now painful.

"Ben?" Then I remember he was going surfing.

I sit with my head in my hands for a while. What happened? I remember Jess telling me to go home. Then? What? A lot of green drink and dancing. Ben had already gone when I came back into the room. It was still dark, but what the time was I have no idea. I remember chucking up in the pot plants downstairs. I check my wallet—empty, but I still have a couple of hundred thousand rupiah in my pocket—about twenty bucks, in small notes. What time is it now? I find my phone. The glass is cracked—how did that happen? I flick it on and it flashes '2:50' briefly, then it fades to black. Afternoon?

I feel like crap. I can smell myself. I sit in my clothes under the shower with a spray of cold water on me. I vainly try and scrub the green vomit stain from the front of my T-shirt, but I am too weak. I drink the water from the shower because I haven't got any bottled water. My thirst is killing me.

I think of Jess. What a disaster. I really made an idiot of myself. I was so pissed she and her mates had run away from me as fast as they could. Who can blame them? What a dickhead! My head thumps painfully and I daren't make any fast movements. I am starving because I haven't eaten since for ever, but the thought of food makes me want to puke again. I peel my wet things off and struggle into dry clothes without drying myself and try to open the door, but the bright light outside pierces my skull like a sword so I allow myself to fall back on the bed. I push the green stained pillow onto the floor and grab Ben's. A few minutes rest and …

13.

"Hey Ras, you sick mongrel, this room stinks."

When I open my eyes, I can see the mask of distaste on Ben's face, even behind the layer of white sunscreen across his nose. I moan in response and roll towards the wall. A few minutes later I can hear him in the shower, singing softly to himself. It all sounds normal and healthy, so I make the effort to sit up. Not too bad. My head doesn't ache as much anymore—but I think someone installed a lead weight just behind my eyes while I was asleep. I think of food. The thought makes me feel ill again, but I am so hungry it is almost painful.

"You had dinner?" I call out through the door. My voice is raspy. It's the first time I have used it today—apart from moaning.

"What?"

"Dinner," I say loudly.

"Okay, give us five and I'll be ready."

But I can't wait. I need water really badly. "I'll see you in the restaurant. I am going down."

"What?"

But it's too hard to reply.

It is dark outside—where has the day gone? Gingerly I climb down the stairs and walk past the pool to the restaurant. I check my phone. There are no messages, but maybe it's broken. It doesn't seem to be getting a signal.

The waitress brings me two small bottles of water and I drink both of one of them straight away. I am looking at the menu when Ben comes down.

"What looks good, mate?" he asks.

"It all looks like crap to me right now. But I am starving. I could eat a horse."

"Ask them," Ben chuckled. "They may have one here somewhere."

I settle on nasi goreng special. Ben chooses chicken and orders a Bintang.

"You want a beer?" he asks me. My stomach churns.

"Not today, probably never again," I say.

Ben is buoyant. He's had a great day down in Uluwatu. He says the surf is the best it's been for years. He's feeling great and, not for the first time, I wonder what it's like to love something as much as he does.

"What have you been up to, mate? Looks like you've come off second best?"

And so, I tell Ben about my activities last night. Well, everything I can remember. It takes a few minutes and then I tell him that I think I've blown my chance with Jess.

"Ah well," he says without pity. "Plenty more fish and all that ... but what about The Invigilator? What are you going to do about him?"

"I dunno."

"I mean, I only ask because I think he's sitting behind you," he says, pointing his chin. "Isn't that him?".

What? Has he been listening? I spin around to where Ben is pointing and see Invigilator Man and Redface sitting at a table across the other side of the restaurant. They both have large Bintangs in front of them and they're chatting quietly. But he's too far away to have heard me and I am relieved.

"So, he's still here then. I hope Jess is alright ... should I call the police?"

"For what. Don't be a moron. He hasn't done anything has he?"

I think for a second. "No, you're right. We'll just have to watch him."

"We?" says Ben. "Keep me out of your hair-brained schemes. I am going to bed."

Invigilator Man was getting up to leave.

"I am going to follow him," I say.

"You're an idiot," Ben says. "See you tomorrow."

Invigilator Man goes out in the street, leaving Redface to finish his beer. I wait a few seconds then I am after him. I can easily spot his tall stooping figure among the crowd in Poppies Lane and I walk about twenty metres behind him. Poppies Lane is a one-way street, but motorcyclists get around the one-way system by riding the wrong way down the footpath and several times I have to jump onto the road to avoid them. Invigilator Man goes into a Circle-K minimart and through the window I see him buying a few items—some biscuits, water and an ice-cream. He spends a few minutes chatting to the young girl on the checkout. I hide in the shadows across the road, then follow him back to the hotel. He sits back down with Redface.

So much for my sleuthing, I give up. Ben is right, I am being an idiot. My head hurts. I go upstairs to our room. Ben chuckles when he sees me. "That didn't take long," he says.

14.

I wake up feeling okay, but quickly remember that I have wasted a whole day because of that stupid green drink and lost my chance with Jess. It's all down the gurgler—she'll never talk to me again, I reckon. And who can blame her?

Ben is packing his surfing gear and getting ready to go. It's already light so maybe he's slept in.

"No," he says. "I looked up the surfing app and the waves won't be here until 10. What are you doing today? Want to come to Uluwatu? I got my own bike now."

I think for a while. Jess is a lost cause; she won't talk to me now.

"Okay," I say. "But I can't surf …"

"It doesn't matter, you can hang out on the cliff and watch. It'll be great. Come on, let's go."

So, I find myself on the back of Ben's hired motorbike. His surfboard is in a special rack welded to the bike's frame. The traffic is terrible. We come out of Kuta at a huge intersection wrapping around a magnificent white statue of rearing horses, frozen in a moment of extreme activity. There are cars and bikes everywhere, but Ben is a surprise. He deftly steers the little Honda though any gap he sees and weaves through the traffic effortlessly. We're the fastest on the road and he's doing really well. I am thinking how bikes are the best way to travel and dreaming of buying my own back in Darwin, when we stop at traffic lights and I look left at the bloke on the bike beside us. The skin of his left arm and leg is grazed and bleeding and scratches on the bike tell me he's recently come off.

"You all right?" I call across to him. He grimaces in pain.

"Ya," he says. He must be German. "I have to be more careful, ya?"

We move off with the green light and is it me, or is Ben now riding a little slower than before? Taking more care? Good idea, I think. Dad said there's an entire industry out of Asia that no one ever talks about. It moves dead and injured tourists back to their home countries. He says lots of people have motorbike accidents, drink poison alcohol or catch nasty diseases and end up going home in body-bags.

"Stick to beer," he had warned me about drinking, before I left home. "There's no methanol in that." I shake my head at the thought, remembering my wayward fling on green booze the other night. Methanol makes you blind, or brain damaged … or dead, and I don't want that. Lots of tourists and locals are damaged here every year from crap booze.

Anyway, he bought me some travel insurance as a present before I left home, though I don't know if it covers motorbike accidents or drunken idiocy.

It takes another half hour to reach Uluwatu. The traffic gets less and less as we get nearer. Only surfers come down here, I reckon.

Ben parks the bike among a bunch of others and unties his board.

"We go down that path to nearly the bottom, then up to that café there. You see it? He says. "That's where the good views are and they do the best banana milkshakes."

A couple of other blokes arrive with their boards and Ben says g'day to them by name. We walk down the path and cross a little bridge, before climbing up the other side. We meet a few other people and Ben seems to know everyone.

"Everyone's friendly here," he says. "It's a pretty good vibe."

There are only two or three others in the café, sitting on wooden benches looking out across the sea. They all say hello when we enter. The view is magnificent, the ocean is so blue and bright I am glad I am wearing my sunnies. Half a dozen surfers are out on the water, but the waves aren't good, Ben says. "Wait a while, the swell will arrive soon and then you'll see some action."

"Where're you from?" asks a surfer with an Irish accent. He is tall, darkly tanned and lean, but his huge shoulders and arm muscles remind me of the big red kangaroos I saw once in the desert back home—he must surf all the time.

"Darwin," I reply. "Just here for a few days?"

"Ahh," he understands. "A schoolie, like Ben?"

Ben has been watching the sea while plastering sun-cream on his face and neck and he now points with his chin. "Here they come. I'll see you soon. I am going." And sure enough, the set of waves coming in now are beauties, standing tall as they curl over before crashing in on themselves, like a huge ocean zipper being closed across the water. I am amazed at how quickly conditions have changed. One bloke is already riding a wave and he disappears behind a wall of water, before shooting out of the barrel, followed by a burst of spray.

All the surfers in the café are grabbing their boards and heading down. I tag along behind Ben, curious. We reach the water's edge and I am amazed to see we are in a canyon and can't see out much at all. The sea is washing up and down the tiny beach but there's a huge wall of rock in front of us. The surfers jump on their boards and paddle out to sea under it, through a tunnel, and I lose sight of Ben straight away. It seems the only place to watch him surf is back on the cliff in the café, so I climb back up.

There are about twenty people out on the water now. The waves are coming in, one after another and each surfer waits patiently for the wave that has his or her name on it. A girl with long blond hair rides a wave right in from way out. For a moment she looks like Jess and butterflies flap in my guts, but it's not her.

I order a banana milkshake and sit in the sun watching them. Ben is as good at surfing as the rest of them—I feel proud of my friend.

Apart from the waitress and someone inside the kitchen I am alone, the only one not surfing. The milkshake is really good and I order a second. I am thinking of getting a third when a bunch of guys come up together from the sea.

They've caught some good waves and are happy and excited. They stand their boards along the wall outside and come in and order milkshakes and hamburgers, although one orders some Indonesian food—a nasi goreng special. His mates tease him about "going local."

Then they sit around me on the benches, chatting about the waves.

One of them asks me,

"What do you reckon? You ever seen better barrels than this in Bali? It's really pumping here at the moment."

I agree. "They are magnificent." And we sit there chatting about surfing together and they start sharing jokes.

"How do surfers say "hello" to each other?" says one. "They wave!" and we all groan good naturedly.

"How can you spot a surfer at a wedding? He's the one that's not there," says another.

I don't know any surfing jokes except Ben did say once that surfing is the only sport where you can pee whenever you want. "That's why they call them wetsuits," he said.

I repeat it and that gets a good laugh. "The old jokes are the good jokes, Ras," says a bloke in board shorts hung so low his pubic hair is showing. Now that's a fashion I will never understand …

We are getting on really well. I order a hamburger for lunch. Ben will be back soon, I think.

Then one of the surfers says,

"Hey Ras, what sort of board do you ride?"

"Who, me?" I say. "I can't surf, never tried."

It's as if a tap has been turned off. Within a few minutes everyone is sitting on the benches at the far end of the café and no one talks to me again. Shit, what did I say? But then Ben comes back and joins me.

"Ah, don't worry about them," he says. "If you're not a surfer they don't want to know you. They're wankers ...up themselves."

Ben orders a hamburger and I notice that it's already two o'clock. By the time the burger arrives, and he's eaten it, it's after three and, as there's no more waves today, we go back to his bike and head back to the hotel.

The traffic is even worse though Tuban to Kuta now, although it's a little quicker in the one-way flow of traffic along Kuta beach. It seems to take ages to get to Poppies Lane. We pull into the little motorbike parking spot next to our hotel reception and climb off feeling stiff and sore. Ben unties his board and we walk through the restaurant to get to our room. I notice Invigilator Man and Redface at a table on the side, drinking

Bintangs. They're just sitting, watching the world pass by outside. Invigilator man's claw hand is wrapped like a bunch of sticks around his bottle and Redface is resting his on his mountainous belly. They both look pretty relaxed.

"Weirdos!" I mutter. Invigilator Man looks like one of those bobbing bird desk toys that ducks up and down into a glass of water.

Ben and I take turns in the shower and clean up. About six o'clock we are ready for food and head down Poppies 2 to a little restaurant, called Fajar Resto, for dinner. It's packed by both Indonesians and tourists and Ben says that's a sign of good food and he always eats here when he comes to Bali. As if to prove it the waitress says, "Hello Ben, long time, no see."

"Hi, Ibu Aya," he replies. "This is my friend, Ras."

We shake hands and Ibu Ayu leads us to a small table. We have to squeeze through the other customers sideways to reach it. It has a dark blue plastic tablecloth, a plastic dispenser for thin paper serviettes, and a greasy little basket holding salt, toothpicks, a small plate of chopped fresh chillies and two bottles of sauce: one is black and evil looking, the other is ordinary tomato sauce. I notice someone has wiped the table clean, but lazily, because I can see wipe marks skirting around the serviettes and the basket, as if they'd been too heavy to move. The tables aren't numbered, but a coke company had provided plastic stands with digital eights on them as part of their advertisement. Someone was supposed to colour in the parts of the eight which are not used to make other numbers, but no one has bothered, so every table is number 88.

A TV with lousy reception is mounted on the wall. The sound is on, but what with the conversations all around us and the growls and whines of motorbikes passing in the lane just a few meters away, it just adds to the cacophony—and surely no one is watching it, anyway. The ceiling is cavernous and painted black, like a seedy nightclub, and a dozen fans spin from their wall mounts. Crappy artworks of waterfalls and deer hang in simple frames on the walls.

Ibu Ayu sends over a tired looking waitress who says hello and Ben and I both say 'beer' together, then look at the menu she has brought, while she goes to fetch some Bintang, and we both order chicken and rice when she returns.

Across the road is a kebab shop. They say their kebabs are cooked the "Aussie way" but neither Ben nor I can guess what that means. A spirit house, wrapped in a black and white chequered cloth, has lazy curls of incense smoke waving at us across the road. Next to it is the Harmony Spa, which claims to offer the best massage in town for about six dollars. Two bored looking girls in neat blue uniforms sit in front of it.

"You'd think if it was the best massage in Bali, they'd have some customers," I say, and Ben laughs.

"They all say that," he says. "There are massage spas everywhere, with every style of massage. I saw one today that offers "sunburn massage", which you'd think can't be very pleasant."

A girl at the next table is talking about an Australian schoolie who got arrested in Sky Garden by the Balinese police for drugs. She said he was caught with a little packet of white powder he had bought.

Ben catches her attention and asks her what has happened to him.

"The security guards grabbed him and took him to the police station. They've locked him up. They say he'll be in gaol for fifteen years if he's guilty. Stupid dickhead,' she said. "What a way to wreck your life. He is eighteen! It was probably a set-up too; they reckon there are always plain clothes police watching the crowd."

Her friends all agree. I tell them about the guy who had tried to sell me ecstasy the other night at Sky Garden—maybe I was being setup then. Phew, I think, lucky! Then I remember the green vomit episode I also survived. *Really lucky*, I conclude.

Ben starts talking with the girl's friends about surfing and soon all five of us are sharing a table and chatting and laughing, drinking beer. Ben and the guys tell more surfer jokes, some of which are new to me and some I don't understand. I decide to try and remember one or two, just in case I end up on the cliff above Uluwatu again.

"Why didn't the surfer ride the glassy waves?" asks the girl.

"Why?" we all chorus.

"Because he heard they were breaking!"

And we all groan together. Perhaps some of these jokes aren't worth remembering after all.

And so, the evening goes. It's late when Ben pays the bill because I have nearly run out of rupiah, saying I owe him, and we farewell our new friends. Then we wander back to the hotel. On the way we stop off at the curved front wall of Tubes Bar in Poppies Lane because it looks like a huge wave. It has a surfboard imbedded into it and Ben stands on it in a surfing pose and gets me to take a picture with his phone. I have a go too— it's as close as I'll get to a real wave, I reckon, and it'll look cool on Facebook. Ben and I have no desire to go to the nightclubs. We have had a great night, anyway—all you need is friends.

15.

I count my remaining rupiah. Nearly everything I changed three days ago is gone. I'll have to change more dollars this morning and I extract some from the secret hiding place in my bag, feeling like an idiot for bringing everything in cash—Ben said my ATM card will work in the machines here and I could just extract money when I needed it, without risking losing the lot. It's something I should have checked before leaving home. Plus, I'll have to be more careful with how much I spend—Bali hasn't been a cheap holiday at all, so far. I am suddenly sad when I remember the motorbike I was going to buy. It took me ages to save up this cash. What a fool I have been!

Ben has gone surfing again, before dawn. We had a good time last night. But, alone again, I sigh and wander out to the restaurant for breakfast. Invigilator Man and Redface are having theirs near the front entrance, so I choose a table near the back, beside the pool, and sit where I can see them, but I am not really interested any more. I feel strange and deflated, as if all the fight has gone out of me. I have been thinking things about Invigilator Man that were bad, but what evidence did I really have? Only his creepy behaviour in the exam and the photo of Jess in a bikini. Perhaps it wasn't her, after all, but some model he'd downloaded from the net … although I am sure he said the name 'Jess'. And I did see him coming out of the Agung the other day …

Ah well … I am eating an 'American Breakfast' which is completely unsatisfying, but I feel that it's what I deserve as punishment. The toast is soggy, the egg leathery and the orange juice seems to be missing any orange. I try to work out a plan for the day—change money first, wander around the shops, buy some DVDs, maybe see a movie, have dinner with Ben if he's back this afternoon, maybe a few beers. Depressing! Perhaps I'll take up surfing.

I finish the fake orange juice and go out onto Poppies Lane. I remember that up the street in Legian there's a whole lot of shops advertising money changing services at a better rate than the official places, so I head that way. Ben has warned me that they'll be rip-offs, but it's worth a try I guess—I need as many rupiah as I can get.

I pass the Agung on the other side of the road and wonder wistfully what Jess is doing. Further along there's a bloke outside his shop with a long stick with some bent wire tied to it. He's using it to hook up hangers with T-shirts on them as a display for his shop, but I see a 'change money sign' near his door showing really good rates.

"You change Australian dollars?"

"Yes," said the man. "Come inside."

I follow him into his shop, pushing through the rows of T-shirts and cheap souvenirs he displays on packing boxes along the walls. It doesn't look as though he sells many, a lot of this crap is really dusty. There is a little counter in the dark near the back, which he sits behind. It all seems a little gloomy, and not just because there's not much light.

"How much?" he asks. He seems bored— he must do this all day.

"A hundred," I put two fifty-dollar notes on the counter.

He gets out a calculator and does a quick calculation and shows me how many rupiah I will get. Then he gets out wads of blue fifty thousand rupiah notes and makes a big show of counting them out on the counter. At 'one million' I reach for the pile because he has started a second.

"No, don't touch," he says, and starts speaking rapidly in Indonesian. He looks so intently at me I daren't look away, but there's a quick movement of his hand. Did he just sweep some of the notes back in the drawer? I am suddenly suspicious. He finishes counting and puts the notes together.

"Let me count it too," I say.

"Why? You saw me count!" he says. Now I am sure he's dodgy. I take my hundred dollars back off the counter.

"I need to count it myself," I say.

"Go away, I will not do business with you," he replies, looking offended. I turn quickly then and get out, with my heart pounding. Back in the bright sunshine I laugh. What a buzz—and I still have my money.

I walk down Legian a bit. There are more money changers down this way, all with the same rate—higher than the banks. I wonder if they're all crooks. Maybe I should try another one, just for fun …

"Ras … Ras …" calls a voice.

16.

It's Jess. I have been so preoccupied I didn't notice her. She runs up to me.

"Hi," she says. "Where have you been? I've been worried about you. You don't answer your phone. We looked everywhere for you yesterday. Where were you for the last two days?"

"What … why?" I ask.

"Because we left you the other night when you had too much to drink …"

"Eh?"

" …and my father says we were irresponsible to leave you. I told him all about it. He says kids on Schoolies have to look out for each other—especially if their parents aren't around."

"Um …?"

"Yes. I told him what happened and he was really cross with me and told me to go out and look for you. Oh, Ras, anything could have happened to you. I was thinking I'd have to ring your mum …"

We are standing in the hot sun on the footpath, so we duck into a nearby frozen-yoghurt place and I am really glad it is air-conditioned. As I don't have any rupiah, Jess buys me a drink.

Jess asks me where I've been and what happened and I had to admit I was so sick on Sunday I stayed all day at the hotel, and yesterday, I went surfing with Ben. And I had broken my phone.

"Oh, you poor thing …" Does she mean me or the phone, I wonder?

"It was this green stuff they sell, an alcoholic Kermit the Frog in a blender …" I say.

And then we laugh and chat about being in Bali. Jess says that she and Lou had looked in every hotel in Poppies Lane for me yesterday but didn't know which one mine was. Today Lou had gone to the Lion Safari Park with Ivana and Trevor and her father, who was staying somewhere in Kuta too. Jess had decided to stay behind to see if she could find me. When she tells me this my heart soars. A second chance!

We go back onto Jalan Legian and I find an official money changer to get some rupiah.

I tell her about the crooked money changer I had met that morning. As we walk back towards the Agung, Jess tells me she thought I was brave venturing into dodgy places. I just giggle, until I realise that when she says 'brave' what she really means is 'stupid'.

Jess's phone rings.

"Oh hi, Daddy," she says. "I found Ras … yes, everything is fine … his phone is broken … ok …yes … alright then … love you."

"What do you want to do today?" she asks me.

"I dunno … how about the beach? Or the cinema … or both?"

"Well the beach is too polluted—you can smell the sewerage! We can swim at the pool in my hotel."

"Or mine," I say. "I haven't been in it yet. But your pool will be nicer. What say I jog back to my hotel and get my swimmers and see you there in twenty minutes?"

"Okay, Ras, I'll wait for you by the pool."

I arrive at her hotel in less than ten minutes and she's already lying in the sun on a pool lounge in her red bikini. I try not to stare. Act cool! I tell myself, and fuss with the giant blue and white striped hotel towel Jess has collected for me from the booth. A huge umbrella shades the table beside us and we order some juices and chips for a snack and, after a while, some lunch.

We spend all afternoon there, swimming and chatting. I have never been happier than this.

I think of Invigilator Man and am comfortable enough to ask Jess if she's been hassled by strangers whilst she's been here.

"Nobody any stranger than you were the other night." We both laugh.

"I am sticking to beer from now on," I promise.

I am relieved. In the back of my mind I've been worried about her. While I was sick, I couldn't protect her and yesterday I abandoned her when I went with Ben to Uluwatu. Then I think that's all nonsense—it's not as if we're a proper couple or anything. But all those strange feelings of wanting to look after her have come back. Luckily, she's clearly not seen Invigilator Man.

We talk about the kid who has been arrested for buying drugs at Sky Garden. It was on the same night we were there. I tell her that someone had offered to sell me some too, but I told him to piss off.

Jess feels sorry for the bloke, even though she doesn't approve of drugs at all.

"A Balinese gaol can't be a nice place to spend fifteen years," she says, and I agree.

"Anyway, the guy's parents have just flown in to see what they can do".

"Imagine how worried they are," she adds.

Her phone rings again:

"Hi Lou. How were the lions? … great … fish, yes … Nyoman's place, you remember it? Yes, see you there … seven … bye."

"Are you joining us for dinner?"

"Yes, sure, of course" I reply, disappointed it won't be just us two.

"Great. It's my last night in Bali. The time has gone fast, I can't believe it. We go home tomorrow afternoon."

"Shame," I said. "I go home on Friday. I guess I'll hang around with Ben again."

Jess asks me what I am going to do when I get home.

"Well," I say. "I'll have to wait for my results—to see if my ATAR will get me into CDU. But I'll be able to work at my cleaning job, maybe find another job to earn some extra cash for a couple of months—I am going to buy a motorbike when I have the money …"

"Cool," say Jess. "We can go for a ride somewhere."

And there it is, as simple as that. Jess wants to see me when we're back in Darwin. My heart leaps.

It's already nearly five. I suggest I go back to my hotel, shower and change, then pick her up, just before seven. She said Nyoman's Restaurant was about five minutes in a taxi, so that would work out fine.

I stroll back to Poppies Lane and my hotel, smiling at the street touts. Nothing will spoil my day now. Ben is in the room, tired but happy after a day on the waves.

"I am going out for dinner with Jess!" I boast. "We've had the best day."

"Onya, ya mongrel, that's the way," says Ben. "I am going out for a few beers with the boys later. Maybe catch you after dinner?"

"Don't count on it," I grin.

17.

This time I am perfectly on time and, in fact, have to wait a few minutes for Jess. She walks out of the hotel looking beautiful in a simple white sundress that swirls around her and shows off her shoulders and neck. Her golden hair is plaited and twisted around the back of her head, but a few stray strands fall across her cheek, framing her dark eyes. Two delicate golden earrings hang from her perfect ears and tiny jewels in a thin gold chain around her neck flash red and green as she turns. I catch her scent like before—flowers wafting on the breeze. I feel weak. I don't know what to say.

"Wow," is all that comes out.

She smiles and hooks the stray hair back over her ear. "Get a taxi will you, Ras."

She tells the driver where to take us. The traffic down Jalan Legian is slow—all going one way, but bumper to bumper in a single lane. It is Monday night. Jess asks the taxi driver why it is so busy and he replies in rapid Indonesian.

"He says this is Jalan Legian, and it's always busy here," Jess translates for me.

We are a few minutes late when we arrive at Nyoman's Restaurant, but I am disappointed not to spend longer in the taxi—Jess held my hand most of the way. I am over the moon.

Huge posters of cooked fish are displayed along the walls on the front. They can be seen from the beach. The restaurant is open to the air but there's also an enclosed glass-windowed room up the back—that must be the air-conditioned section, I think. There's a charcoal fire burning in a metal trough in the front and a chef is barbecuing saté sticks of squid and vegetables. Large reef fish are displayed in crushed ice in trays. There's a fish tank full of live blue crayfish and another of freshwater fish; a death row from which customers can choose. Slow jazz drifts across the crowd from a trio on a small stage near the kitchen door. This is a really classy place.

"Um, Jess," I say. "I only changed a hundred dollars. I don't have enough cash to eat here."

"Don't worry about that," she replies. "Come on, let's find the others."

The smell of beautifully cooked fish and spices fills the air. The restaurant is very popular. Everyone is talking and laughing and eating and drinking. Nearly every table is taken and I catch sight of some amazing looking food as we pass. My mouth is already watering. I follow Jess through the tables obediently.

Suddenly my blood freezes. Over Jess's shoulder I see them: Invigilator Man and Redface are sitting at a table right in front of us. And we're about to walk right past them.

I don't think. I instinctively grab Jess's arm and pull her, too roughly, to the left, behind some palms planted in a huge rectangular pot.

"Rasmus, what the hell? What are you doing?" she demands.

"We've got to go. We can't stay here. Now, Jess."

"What the hell has got into you?" Jess hisses.

I decide that maybe it is the time to explain to her the danger she's in.

"Do you remember in the exam, the chemistry, there was this creepy invigilator?" She shakes her head. Her eyes are wide. "No? Well, he's here and he's been hunting you, Jess. He has a picture of you on his phone in your bikini. He's with a fat bloke, and the two of them have been looking for young girls. They're staying at my hotel. They're sickos. He's sitting at a table just over there. Let's get out of here."

Jess looks startled.

"Where?" she Jess. "Point them out."

So, I do, carefully, through the palms, so we're not spotted. Jess looks back at me and studies my face for a while. Then she makes up her mind.

"Come on." She grabs my arm and pushes me in front of her—straight towards Invigilator Man's table!

Oh, no. He's seen us. Jess is going to have it out with him right here, right now. We're there. I am standing like a rabbit in a spotlight. Invigilator Man looks at me. Redface looks at me. Lou, Ivana and Trevor look at me.

"Ras," says Jess, "I'd like you to meet my father ... Daddy, this is Ras."

"Hello Ras, I've been hearing about you." I just stand there. I can't speak. It takes all my strength to pull myself together.

"Um, nice to meet you," I finally force out.

"Sit here," says Jess, indicating the chair right across the table from her father. "Oh, and this is Lou's dad, Frank." Redface turns his great head towards me. His eyes seem small and sunken, but sharp.

"Good evening," says Redface, his magnificent moustache hides his mouth, but it vibrates as he talks. He frowns slightly, thinking. "Have we met already?"

"Er, not really," I reply, my own face as red as his. "But we stay at the same hotel, I think."

"Ah yes, I have seen you there. You're in the next room to me, aren't you?" He turns back to speak with Lou. I steal a glance at Jess, who is sitting on my right. Her dark eyes are dark and shiny. Her lips are pursed together tight, quivering. Her body is trembling, she seems to be having trouble breathing. Concerned, I start to speak—and then I realise that she's laughing. She's bottling it up, but I can tell.

"Are you all right, Honey?" asks her father, and she bursts into a fit of giggles. It's infectious. I start to chuckle with her and soon we are sitting there holding our bellies, tears running down our cheeks, crippled with laughter.

Invigilator Man sits there and watches us closely.

"Teenagers!" he says to Redface, shaking his head. "Who will ever understand them?"

18.

Jess reminds me that it's their last day in Bali. She and her friends, her father and Lou's father all have to be at the airport about two-thirty. I have joined them for breakfast at the Agung again, but so have the fathers! Invigilator Man, Redface and I walked up from our hotel together! I can't believe it. I didn't plan it, but they were just there and we were going to the same place, and we sort of stuck with each other, crossing the road at the same time, dodging the same touts … it was weird.

They had already checked out of our hotel and they carried their bags with them to the Agung, and now they are over at reception paying the bill here. Jess's bag is already packed too.

I am still a little embarrassed about last night, but Jess is nice. As for my old mate, Ben—I regret that I told him about what an idiot I have been. As soon as I blurted it out, I realised that it's going to come back to me for the rest of my life. He won't forget. My bet is he'll remember it at really embarrassing times. He'll probably make a speech at my twenty-first!

"You stupid mongrel," he had said, nearly wetting himself with laughter. "After all that!"

But Jess just thinks I am sweet. Even Invigilator Man thought it was okay:

"I am glad Jess had someone else to look her after here," he had said. He and Lou's dad are in Bali to be out-of-sight chaperones for their daughters, and their friends, just in case they are needed. They are having a holiday as well, by themselves, and have just been around for support. It is just coincidence that we are staying at the same hotel.

Jess looks a million dollars. She has double-plaited her hair and tied a few small white flowers in each plait. Jasmine; there's a huge bush of it near the hotel gate. I can smell them if I lean close to her. She's already had a swim and her wet bikini is showing red through the thin white material of an oversized shirt she has pulled on.

"So, what do you want to do on your last day?" I ask, hoping she'll want to hang out with me by the pool or somewhere again.

"Daddy's buying a statue for our pool at home. We're driving up to where it's being carved. He's shipping it back to Darwin and it should be finished now, so we're going to see it first."

Damn, I think.

"But you can come with us," she gushes. "Come, Ras. We'll have a cool time looking through the factory and checking out the carvings …"

"You might as well," says Lou. "We aren't going. Can't think of anything worse …"

Spending the morning with Invigilator Man isn't my highest priority and shopping for statues sounds really boring but, if I want to hang out with Jess, it looks as though I have no choice. So, I agree and hope that Jess doesn't spot my disappointment that we'll be with her father.

Invigilator Man and Redface come back. Invigilator Man stoops over half the table in the process of sitting down and Redface knocks it forward a few inches with his belly. Can't help but notice these two, I think.

"All done," says Invigilator Man. "But gee, you ran up a bit on pool service yesterday, Honey."

"Oh Daddy," says Jess sweetly. "It was just a few chips." I feel her foot nudging me under the table. It hadn't occurred to be yesterday that there'd be a bill. I keep quiet.

Lou and Trevor have been busy on their iPad, reading the news on Facebook.

"That kid who got arrested for drugs at Sky Garden the other day is in all the news," says Lou. "His parents have just flown in from Perth."

"Serves him right," says Redface. "Should know better that meddle with drugs in Bali. They have the death penalty here you know."

"Come on, Frank," says Invigilator Man. "He's just a kid. His whole life is ahead of him. He's made a mistake, sure. But he could get years in the Bali gaol. Do you think he really deserves that?"

"If he's stupid enough to do drugs then I have got no time for him. Can't say he wasn't warned. There are signs up everywhere in the airport and those guys who were executed last year were in the news every day. You'd have to be living under a rock to not understand the risks you take here. That's all I am saying."

The rest of us just sit there. These old blokes don't want our opinion and they rattle on for ages about the idiocy of it all.

"Some of these kids will never learn ..." says Redface. "Lock 'em in gaol and throw away the key."

Invigilator Man is worried about the kid and his parents. He seems to be a nicer bloke than Redface.

"His poor parents. They must be going through hell," he says.

"Listen, Drug-boy bought some white powder in a little plastic bag and the police found it and arrested him. End of story. The parents should have taught him better," Redface is immovable.

"But everyone makes a mistake, yeah sure, you can have a penalty, but fifteen years in gaol? Or execution? For a kid? Punishments here are too harsh."

"What do you think the white powder is?" I ask, remembering my own father's warnings. If I was into drugs would his warning have made any difference the other night?

"The Jakarta Post says it's being tested. Who knows? Cocaine, ecstasy ... That's why they have to test it," says Invigilator Man.

Redface just scoffs. "Serves him right," he repeats. "Drug-boy will be middle-aged by the time he gets back to Perth. If he was smuggling drugs, he'd be for the firing squad."

Jess changes the subject. "Hey Daddy, Ras wants to come with us to see the carving."

Invigilator Man swings his head around to look at me like it's on a boom operated by someone behind him. His hooded eyes gaze at me.

"Really, why?"

Because your daughter is really hot and I really like her, I think. But I say:

"I've never seen a stone carving factory before. It'll be very interesting." I fight the impulse to call him 'Sir'.

"Hmmph," he grunts, but he seems to agree and we concentrate on finishing breakfast for a while, because it is already past nine and Invigilator Man's appointment with the carver is at ten.

"We will take our luggage and head straight to the airport afterwards. You can make your own way back from there," he tells me. "When do you go home?"

"On Friday," I say. I am not looking forward to two days alone in Bali without Jess …

19.

The driver opens the car boot and we pile Jess's and her father's luggage into it. The driver helps arrange the bags. He's a short man, with dark skin and a gold filling in his teeth. He's wearing the regulation Bluebird taxi uniform shirt and black trousers.

"Very good," he says. "Very good." I think that's his only English. His red rubber thongs catch my attention and I look at his feet. Odd. He has an extra toe. I take a second look. Yes, he has six toes. And six more on the other foot. Twelve toes! It's polydactylism! We learned about it in biology.

Oh no, I am distracted. Invigilator Man is about to sit in the back seat of the Bluebird with Jess. That would leave me sitting in the front by myself. I don't want that. But at the last minute he stands aside for her to get in first and I duck around to the other side of the taxi and get in behind the driver. Invigilator Man gives me a look but has no choice but to get in the front of the car. Jess and I share a smile as we settle into the back seat. Her father has to fold himself almost double to get in and he pushes the seat back as far as it can go. His knees are sticking up like fence posts and his head scrapes the ceiling. For a moment I feel a little sorry for him—there's plenty of room in the back.

He asks Jess to give the driver the directions in her good Indonesian.

The taxi joins the one-way traffic down Legian until we get to Bimo Corner, where the bigger roads start, and we zigzag through the traffic to Sunset Drive, and from there to the bypass, which takes us out past Sanur and towards Ubud.

"Did you notice this guy's feet?" I ask Jess quietly enough to not be heard in the front.

"Who?"

"The driver …"

"No," she admits. So, I tell her about his extra toes.

"Weird, eh?"

It's comfortable in the back seat with Jess and I sneak my hand over to hold hers. But

Invigilator Man swings his crane-head around to talk to her and I pull it back guiltily.

The stone carver's factory is among a hundred other factories, exactly like his, on a long sloping road. When we get there, an elderly man approaches and bows to us.

"Selamat Pagi, Pak Manton," he says. "We are nearly ready."

So, we follow him into his factory. All around are statues made of stone, or concrete that looks like stone, which I guess is a bit cheaper. Some are grotesque figures of mythical monsters or Balinese gods. Jess spots a stone kangaroo behind a pile of carved bathroom sinks.

"Let's find the weirdest statue," I suggest.

Jess and I start looking around the place, whilst her father goes with the man to see the statue he has commissioned. The weirdest statue doesn't take long to find. Among the gods, elephants, big breasted nudes and Garudas, I find a huge statue of a turd.

"Hey, look at this," I call her over. "It's a giant turd."

"Don't be crude," Jess tells me. "It's just concrete waste that's been piled there."

I take another look.

"Yeah, I guess you're right. Still, they'd probably sell it if someone wanted it."

Jess hears her father calling and we join him at the back. He is standing beside an incredible statue carved out of black lava. It is of a beautiful girl standing two meters tall with a water jug, out of which water will soon fall into Invigilator Man's swimming pool. She has long wavy hair over her shoulder and flowers and a sarong tied around her waist. Looking closely, I can see the artist has even carved a delicate pattern into the sarong. It surely is a magnificent piece of art.

"Most of the carvings in stone you get in Bali are actually concrete and made partly in a mould. This one is all stone," said Invigilator Man. "It has taken Bapak Made nearly six months to make. Beautiful, isn't it?"

We have to agree. Invigilator Man's eyes are shiny with excitement.

"Meet Saraswati, goddess of knowledge and education," he explains. "Just the thing for an old school teacher like me." Then he turns to Pak Made and speaks rapidly in Indonesian. They have an in-depth conversation. I am stunned. I've only heard him ask Jess to speak Indonesian on his behalf and I say so to Jess.

"Oh, he gets me to talk for him for the practice. Daddy's Indonesian is much better than mine. We used to live in Java when I was a baby. He's organising for its transport to Darwin. Don't ask him how much it's costing, carving like this is really expensive. Mum's going to kill him!"

Back in the taxi, Invigilator Man says he's very pleased and reckons the statue will arrive in Darwin in about six weeks. He doesn't seem to notice that I was clever enough to bags the back seat with Jess like before. He's stuck in the front again, with his knees jacked up to about the level of his ears. And anyway, he's busy sorting through his passport and tickets, making sure he's got everything for the airport.

I ask Jess what she's going to do in Darwin when she gets home. She pauses.

"Oh, just hang around till my ATAR comes through. Then I'll know what university I can get into and start making plans then. I want to go to Melbourne Uni."

Sadness weighs down on me. We have been at school together for three years, but never spoke. I thought Jess was out of my league but, now we've left school, suddenly we're together and she's about to go to Melbourne. Together? Are we? I suddenly wonder if Jess is feeling the way I am. Can I call her my girlfriend? How can I find out? I struggle for words to bring it up. I watch as she tucks a lose strand of hair behind her ear. She sees me watching and smiles. What is she thinking? But Invigilator Man starts talking about his statue again, and the moment passes, and then we're passing through the entrance gate of the airport.

20.

I get a trolley as soon as we're out of the taxi. A dozen porters have turned up to help, but I thank them and say I'll get the bags. What else can I do? They hardly have any luggage anyway. Jess says she's hungry and we go up the ramp to the departure level of the airport and, as we've plenty of time, we stop at La Place Juice Bar and buy expensive mango smoothies and sandwiches. Invigilator Man pays, even though I half-heartedly offer.

We sit at a table with a great view down two floors to the crowd below, waiting outside the arrival hall. Dozens of hotel men wait behind a fence and hold up signs or cards displaying people's names. Some are using selfie sticks to get their signs higher. There must be two hundred of them down there, but mostly blokes—there's only a few women among them. I mention that meeting guests in Bali seems to be a male dominated profession.

The arrival doors open and a buzz of excitement goes through the crowd as a new batch of travellers arrive, pushing their luggage, or carrying surfboard bags over their shoulders. They appear for a few seconds, then disappear as they follow the path though the final duty-free shopping opportunities. Hopeful travellers scan the name cards as they pass until they see their names. I can see a sense of relief wash over them by their smiles, when they meet their contacts. Then they're in Bali proper. Those who haven't been met are immediately set upon by drivers who will drive them wherever they want to go, saying either "transport" or "where you go?", or they wave their hands in front of them, miming driving a car. The blue batik uniform shirts of the Bluebird Taxi company are chief among them.

Invigilator Man gets up and goes to the Periplus Bookshop for something new to read. Jess and I watch the newcomers, amused at how quickly some get cranky after saying no, over and over again. I remember that was how I reacted too. The most persistent, or most annoying, drivers seem to get the fares though and we start guessing who will be successful next.

"Damn and bugger," Invigilator Man is back and obviously upset. "Shit, shit, shit …"

"Daddy, what's happened?" asks Jess.

"I've gone and lost my flippin' passport is what," he says. "Damn," his face contorts in his fury. He collapses back into his chair. "Must have left it somewhere. I have checked my bag. Here's yours, but mine is gone."

"Oh, Daddy, no … what …"

My first though is great, now Jess will stay another day or two. But no …

"You'll just have to go without me, Honey. I can go to the consulate tomorrow. It shouldn't be hard to replace in Bali. Tell Mum I'll be back soon … No, I'll call her later … Frank and Lou will be inside the airport already, so tell them. How can I be so stupid? I checked it in the taxi."

I remember seeing him go through his papers and the passports were definitely there.

"The trouble is there's no room in those bloody taxis, maybe it slipped down and I couldn't see it," he said. "That taxi is long gone now."

Uh oh! I think. It's my fault. If I hadn't forced Invigilator Man to sit in the front …

I look down at the crowd of drivers below. They were milling around, waiting for the next batch of fresh arrivals to emerge from the duty-free zone.

"Do you think … maybe he's still here? Maybe he's looking for another fare down there?"

"Doubt it. He's had plenty of time. He's long gone. And do you remember the taxi number? I don't. There are so many drivers. How would you know which one?"

Invigilator Man has given up. It's true, there are many drivers down there.

A little light went on in my brain.

"I have an idea," I say. "It's worth a try. Come on Jess," and she jumps up with me and we're off, leaving Invigilator Man with the luggage, shaking his head, muttering to himself.

We get in the lift.

"What's going on, Ras?"

"Do you remember our driver?" I ask Jess.

"Well, he worked for Bluebird …"

"No. More than that—he has extra toes, remember? What's the bet, if we ask any Bluebird driver, they'll know him? How many twelve-toed drivers can there be in Bali?"

"Brilliant, Ras. Oh, I could kiss you," Jess's eyes were bright with excitement. Great, I think, until I realise it's just an expression.

We race out and across to where a bunch of the Bluebird taxi guys are standing. Jess is a beautiful girl. When she starts talking with one man, there are suddenly twenty there to listen. Then:

"Ya," says one. "Saya tahu. Dia taman saya, Ketut!"

"He knows him," says Jess. Even better— the driver was getting out his phone and calling him. We wait agonising seconds with our crowd of blue-shirted drivers. They have fallen silent in anticipation. The man says something to Jess.

"He says wait. Ketut is looking for it now." A little line appears between Jess's eyebrows.

And then, yes! The crowd is thrilled. High fives are everywhere. White teeth flash as they smile and laugh. Several blokes pat me on the back. These are the people who make newcomers cranky with their offers of transport. I feel guilty, because I got as cranky as the worst, and they turn out to be the friendliest bunch of guys I've yet met in Bali.

"He says Ketut remembers us. He'll be back in ten minutes and we have to wait where he dropped us off. The passport was down the side of the seat."

We go back up to the departure level and wait on the footpath and about fifteen minutes later Ketut arrives in his taxi, his face wide in smile as he waves the passport at us. A woman with a small child is sitting in the back, surrounded by plastic shopping bags. Jess talks with her.

"She was on her way home. I'll pay her fare for her," Jess says, and she gives her two fifty-thousand-rupiah notes and then a bunch of them to Ketut for his trouble. Everyone is happy.

Jess and I then run up the ramp back to her father, who is sitting alone and looking worried. We've been gone twenty or thirty minutes and he brightens considerably when he sees his passport.

"Jess," he says. "You're a genius."

"Not me," she said. "It was all Ras. He knew how we could track down the driver."

Invigilator Man swings his head around to me faster than it's probably healthy for him to do so.

"Ras, my boy," he is effusive and suddenly his arms are wrapped around me and he gives me as much of a bear hug as his snowman arms can provide.

"What can I say?" he says. "Today, you're a hero."

I am embarrassed and have no words, but Invigilator Man is suddenly busy getting everything together. "We have to hurry now; the counter will be closing in a few minutes."

I go with them and say goodbye at the glass doors, where a uniformed guard checks tickets. He only allows passengers through. Invigilator Man shakes my hand and Jess gives me a hug and they turn to go. Her father is in front, looking the other way, when Jess quickly turns back to me and quickly gives me a big kiss. On the lips! Really.

"Told you I could kiss you," she says, her eyes bright. And then she's gone. I watch through the glass doors until her blonde hair disappears around a corner. I replay her farewell over and over in my head.

22.

It is raining. A heavy flood of water has fallen on us like a collapsing brick wall. It thunders on the roof and drowns out all other noise. We are back in Fajar Resto with Ibu Ayu and I have been telling Ben about how we got Invigilator Man's passport back for him. I also nearly told him about *The Kiss*, but the rain started and that's ok, it'll be best not to tell Ben everything. He has too much ammunition against me as it is.

It's amazing rain. Sitting here it's like we could step into a different world just by leaving the restaurant. The wall of water might be a gateway into another dimension. We get tropical rain like this in Darwin, but the roads at home are wide and you can see it coming. Here in this Kuta lane we had no warning—except a few seconds of an increasing roar as it hit neighbouring rooves and then wham! Instant flood. The lane outside is full already and flowing quickly past us and I realise why the step into the restaurant is so high. Anyone still out and about is getting very wet indeed. Most motorbike riders have pulled their bikes as far to the edge of the lane as possible, to get as much shelter as they can. Some are standing patiently in the restaurant, dripping water from plastic ponchos. The waitresses smile and dodge around them carrying more beer and plates of food to the tables. Someone has placed a bucket near the counter, it's already nearly full, from the drips that fall from the ceiling above it.

Then the rain is over as fast as it started, as if someone turned off a giant sky tap. The road starts to drain and within minutes the traffic is back to normal.

"This'll make the sea dirty tomorrow," says Ben. "The drains will empty of rubbish and it'll all wash back on the beach with the tide."

"What are your plans tomorrow?" I ask Ben.

"It's our last full day," he replied. "Maybe I'll just hang out here with you, go shopping, maybe the movies—it only costs five dollars here. What do you reckon?"

"Great, sounds good," I say, and am relieved that he isn't planning on going back to Uluwatu.

I don't fancy hanging out with surfers, who don't like me because I can't surf, again.

We drink another beer and decide on an early night. We head back to our hotel, jumping puddles on the way.

As we pass through the hotel restaurant, I look for Invigilator Man and Redface, until I remember that they've gone home. I almost miss them. Well, not really, but I really do miss Jess.

I fall asleep thinking of her. Her kiss still lingering on my lips.

23.

I wake slowly and lazily. No need to get up early this morning, I think.

"Come on Ras," Ben says. "You can lie in bed when you're dead."

"What?" I look at him. He's been out already. "Where …?"

"I went for a run, did the whole circuit around Kuta. Then I had a swim. Oh, and I took my bike back to the hire place."

"What time is it?"

"It's the beginning of the rest of your life," he says. "Come on down for breakfast …" And with that, he's gone.

I have a quick shower then join him in the restaurant.

It's not late. Ben must have been up with the sparrows. He certainly knows how to get the most out of life. But the shops here don't open until ten, what's the rush?

We have a leisurely breakfast—banana pancakes, coffee and fruit salad.

"You gotta come down and see the beach. I'll show you something," he says when we've finished.

He leads me down the full length of Poppies Lane and we come out on Jalan Pantai Kuta, the beach road. Hundreds of motor bikes are already parked along the other side of the road and the traffic is thick and slowly moving.

"Morning rush hour," suggests Ben. "There was bugger-all traffic when I jogged here this morning. Follow me."

We hustle along the side of the road until we see a gap between the parked bikes on the other side and we walk boldly out into the traffic and straight across.

As soon as we're on the beach a bunch of old ladies zero in on us, offering massages. One of them takes my hand and looks at my fingernails, then draws such a breath of horror that suddenly I think if I don't get an immediate manicure they might drop off.

But Ben leads me away. "There's nothing wrong with your fingernails, Ras," he says, and we head towards the sea, ignoring the guys who try to rent us plastic chairs, which are placed in awkward straight rows under beach umbrellas.

"Look at this."

I look. Kuta Beach is huge. The sea is more than a hundred meters away and the beach extends in both directions for kilometres. At one end there is an aeroplane coming down low over the sea to land on the airstrip that stretches out from the coast like a tongue catching snowflakes. In the distance in the other direction, hotel and bar owners have planted umbrellas in their patch of sand that stand in neat rows like obedient colourful toadstools. Among them are scattered equally brightly coloured bean bags and beach lounges.

Several people are out on surfboards, but the tide is low, the sea is flat and the surf doesn't impress Ben at all.

I have seen beaches before, but Ben hasn't brought me here to see the sand, but what is on it. As far as we can see there is rubbish—the trash of Kuta, which Ben predicted last night would be here after the heavy rain. Most of the rubbish is plastic. There are millions of wrappers, bags, empty water bottles, nappies and everything else we can imagine—all the detritus of Kuta's rubbish-tossing population is here.

"It's disgusting, Ben. What a mess."

"Yeah, hotels with beach frontages will clear up their own little area, but ninety-nine per cent of it will go back out to sea or get buried in the sand. It's the same every time it rains, right across Indonesia. Rubbish washes out like oil slicks from the islands. I saw plastic in the water at Uluwatu every time I was out surfing, even on clear days."

We walk along the sand for a while. Close to us there are people lying on sand-mats in the sun, their bronzed bodies quietly aging in its glare. We see some girls who are so keen on sunbathing they have cleared a little circle of rubbish for their sand-mats and they lie on them like they've landed in an alien crop circle. Weird.

We jump across a shallow stream of brown water flowing across the beach to the sea. It smells really bad, so we don't want to put our feet in it. People are swimming in the waves nearby. They must be soaking in sewerage, but they don't seem to notice. I think about Jess and the day we hung around her pool. Everything was neat and clean there. What a contrast!

"Let's get out of here," I say. "This is too depressing."

We dodge the traffic again and enter the Kuta Beachwalk Mall. Here we find beauty in the form of gardens and fountains and curtains of greenery cascading from each of the curved balconies. There's an art exhibition on an island in the middle of a circular lake-sized pond which we browse through, but I am more interested in the huge white and yellow fish swimming around and under the bridge. If we come back at three o'clock, a sign tells me, we can watch them being fed. There's a Coffee Bean and Tea Leaf cafe nearby and we sit there for a while. I order an expensive cappuccino and Ben, a latte, and we watch the people pass. They're mostly young, but they're not all foreign tourists. I reckon more than half of the shoppers are Indonesians.

"I heard that Indonesian domestic tourism is the fastest growing industry in Indonesia," Ben told me.

"A lot of these shops," says Ben, looking at a map of the mall he'd picked up from the counter, "are the same as in every other mall in Indonesia. Look, there's Victoria's Secret, Haargen Daz Ice-cream, Starbucks, Armani Jeans, Gap, Timberland, Bodyshop. That's the trouble with malls, they're all the same."

"Is there a cinema here?" I ask.

"Yes, top floor."

We go up there to see what's playing.

"There's John Wick, Chapter 2, starting at twelve thirty for fifty thousand rupiah, or if we wait thirty minutes more, we can see it in the premier lounge—it's only seventy-five thousand rupiah."

"What's a Premier Lounge?" I ask.

"Don't know, but it's only a couple of dollars more. Want to try it?"

We buy tickets, and hang around for half an hour, then sit in huge comfy lounge chairs in the most luxurious cinema I have ever seen. Waitresses come and take our order for popcorn and drinks, and we watch John Wicks Chapter 2, even though I have never seen Chapter 1, or even heard of John Wicks, but by the time he has successfully shot up half of Rome without any police showing up, neither of us fancy going back out into the real world, so we watch another movie. This time it's Jackie Chan in 'Kung Fu Yoga'. I don't concentrate much on this movie—I am distracted by thoughts of Rome. It might be fun to go there some day.

We are frittering away our last full day in Bali.

For dinner, we go back to Fajar Resto, and Ibu Ayu and the staff greet us as old friends. Ben meets some of his surfer mates and we get stuck into a few beers with them and eat chicken and cashew nut stew. I don't mention that I can't surf.

One of them, Mac, asks if we have heard the news about the schoolie arrested with the drugs.

"What's happened?" asks Ben.

"Well," says Mac. "They tested the drugs and it turned out to be paracetamol. The guy is now free. He's going back to Perth tomorrow."

We talk about this for ages. Redface had called him 'Drug-boy' and I wonder what he'd say about this—does buying a little plastic zip-lock bag of paracetamol make you a 'drug-boy'?

"He was clearly ripped off," reckons Mac. "He thought he was buying something else."

"I was offered ecstasy on the same night he was arrested at Sky Garden. I didn't see it, but does that come in little plastic bags?"

"Nah, mate," says one of the surfers. "You get it in little blue or white tablets. They have a little crown logo on them." He is very intense with weird eyes. This bloke is clearly an authority, so I don't question him and avoid his gaze. But again, I am relieved I said no to that pusher the other night.

"Sounds like he was lucky that it was a rip-off this time," says Ben. "It kept him out of gaol."

We all agree and conclude that it had probably been a set up from the start.

"It happens all the time," says the surfer with the eyes.

24.

Ben and I drag our bags and his surfboards up the ramp into the airport. Ben says he is hungry and I tell him there's a good juice and sandwich place on the right, at the departure level. At La Place I buy the same food and drink I had before and sit at the same table I shared with Jess. If that sounds soppy, it is only because all the other tables are taken. Really.

Ben sits where Jess sat and we play the game of guessing the next person to accept an offer of transport from the drivers down below, but it's not as much fun with him as it was with Jess.

One of the Bluebird taxi drivers looks up, spots me and waves, and soon a bunch of them are looking up giving me a thumbs up and cheery smiles.

"Well aren't you Mister Popular with the taxi drivers?" says Ben. I wave back.

At the entrance we show our tickets to the guard and join the line to put the boards, and our bags, through the x-ray machine. We collect them again and walk around to the Air Asia check-in counters and line up behind a bunch of scruffy, sun-burned travellers.

We hand in our luggage and get our boarding passes, and have to go through another x-ray machine. I have to take my belt off after it pings the metal detector. I go back and put it in a tray, so it can be x-rayed by itself, and then, holding up my droopy pants, I pass through the detector again and the guard asks me to stand still as he waves an electronic wand around me. That done, with my belt once again around my waist, we line up at Passport Control. Ben watches the lines like a hawk.

"Sometimes a new line opens up and you can dash to the front of it, even if you're at the end of the queue," he says. It is true, a new immigration officer takes his seat, in a booth on the right, and Ben is off like a shot to start the new line. I am slower—there are three or four people in front of me by the time I get there, and Ben is already handing his passport to the official. When my passport is stamped too, we enter the no-man's land of the international departure lounge. It's all very easy and mundane and stress-free, but once again I have learned some travellers' tricks from Ben. His mother is the real expert, he tells me, he's just a beginner.

The delays and the stress of our trip over here are forgotten. I now think I could get used to international travel. Maybe it's time to see the world. I'd like to go to Europe. Rome looked pretty good in that movie yesterday, even if John Wicks has shot it all to hell. Maybe Jess would like to come. As I am thinking this the loud speakers came on, announcing the flight to Rome was now on its last boarding call. I wonder how much would it cost to catch that flight? I'd have to work hard to get the money. I don't even have the cash to buy the duty-free whiskey Dad asked me to get for him, but Ben lends me $30 and I buy a single bottle, which I have to collect at the gate just before we leave.

We have a while to wait. We wander around the duty-free shops and look out the windows at the planes.

"Which gate do we have to go to?" I ask Ben.

"Mum's got this theory. She reckons that Darwin people are the worst dressed travellers that pass through this airport. Let's just tag along behind some blokes in boardies and singlets and double-plugger thongs and I bet we'll get to the right gate without even having to check the board. Want to try?"

"Sure," I say. "How about those daggy blokes there? They look real Darwin"

Three scruffy guys in singlets pass us.

"Yep, I reckon they're Darwin guys for sure," says Ben, and we follow them, as he predicted, to the right departure gate and, within minutes, board the plane. It departs on time and we have two and a half hours of reading and dozing before arriving back in Darwin, ten minutes early.

25.

First thing, Mum takes me to Casuarina Mall to drop off my phone because maybe it can be repaired. I'll have to pay for it or buy a new one. My cash reserves are really low now. Later, I'll call my boss and say I am ready to go back to my cleaning job to build it up the money again and can work even more hours now. He told me the other week that he can give me full-time, for a while, until after Christmas, because it's hard to get workers in the wet season. I'll need cash if I'm going travelling, and if I do two months full-time work, I'll have enough for a good trip. Buying a Honda now seems to me to be a poor second choice. My parents are flabbergasted—but I haven't told them my secret plan.

Mum does a little shopping in Woolies and I wait till we're home again before asking if I can borrow her phone. I didn't want to ring Jess in the car where Mum could listen.

Jess answers on the third ring.

"Hi Jess," I say.

"Ras, you're home. How did it go the last few days?" she says. Normal words, but I sense excitement in her voice.

"Great," I say. "What are you doing today?"

"Oh, just hanging round. Shall we meet? How about at Casuarina, that ice-cream shop? We can do lunch."

So that's what we're going to do. Jess, the hottest, smartest girl from the college, and yours truly, are doing lunch. Really! And I am going to ask her if she wants to come with me to Rome in January. I reckon she'll say yes. She's going to Melbourne when uni starts and I am going to stay here, in Darwin at CDU, but maybe we could see some of the world before the semester starts.

Next year, at uni, we'll be five thousand kilometres from each other. But anything can happen before then and, if we're lucky, it will …